ALL WAYS

ALL WAYS

KELLY COONS

NEW DEGREE PRESS

COPYRIGHT © 2021 KELLY COONS

ALL WAYS

ISBN   978-1-63676-902-8 *Paperback*

978-1-63676-966-0 *Kindle Ebook*

978-1-63730-070-1 *Ebook*

To my brothers.

CONTENTS

———

LETTER FROM
THE AUTHOR

———

"Well, that was to be expected." Is there any phrase in the
English language that is more disheartening? There is a reason
why disappointment is such a powerful deterrent. Anger—
and even sadness—gives energy to work off of. Disappointment, though, is powerful enough to destroy that energy.

For creative ventures, then, which are inherently ener-
gy-consuming, there can be no worse reaction on the part
of the audience than disappointment. Worse than no reaction, disappointment means that there *were* expectations and
there *was* excitement...just that you failed to deliver.

Creators are acutely aware of the threat of disappointment. I don't claim to be unique. But I do think there is
a special type of disappointment when you fail to be the
representation that people are so hungry for.

Autistic people are hungry for representation. I know I am.
I know that's why I'm writing this story. But whether I fail
or not, I know that Autistic people will continue to be hungry for representation. I believe that Autistic representation

benefits both Autistic and Allistic (meaning not Autistic) people, but it is the latter group that needs convincing. And it is the latter group that has both the numbers advantage and the power.

I am Autistic. It is part of my identity. I know that this identity, which is something I cannot change, disables me. But I am not disabled by my autism. I am disabled by my world's lack of accommodation for my autism.

I hope, in reading this book, dear reader, a lot of it looks familiar. Expected, even. Two brothers on a trip. There and back again. A boy who can't wait to grow up; a young man who wants adulthood to slow down. The quest.

Yes, this story should look familiar. I suppose the difference is who is going on this journey.

Autistic characters aren't often allowed to go on a journey. They are allowed to be solitary geniuses. They are allowed to hold pearls of wisdom for a neurotypical character's journey. That is "first wave Autistic representation"—to borrow more language from feminist critique.

I hope that *All Ways* will help usher in a second wave of Autistic representation, where Autistic characters are allowed to be what most people are: neither geniuses nor dependent on others, where Autistic characters can be—dare I say it—*typical*.

As we know from media studies, what characters are allowed to do can dictate what people are allowed to do.

Here is my central struggle: If someone who is not Autistic messes up a story about autism, well, that was to be expected. This is not to say that people outside of a certain marginalized identity cannot have the best intentions or even that they do not have the skill to tackle issues outside of their lived experience. (Here is the secret to creation: Even when we are not building something off our own lived experience, we are drawing upon *someone's*.) It is undeniable, though, that the expectations are different. Disappointment is draining, yes, but at least in messing up representation for something you were never hungry for, you are not disappointing yourself.

So, hello, Past Kelly, this one goes out to you. Because you are not a tragedy. You are not the solitary genius. You are not the accessory to a neurotypical character's "lesson." You have energy: angry energy, sad energy, and, yes, funny energy. You are Autistic. You are typical. The two are not mutually exclusive.

CHAPTER 1

——

A boy hunches over a grave of papers. The posters of The Killers and the soccer jerseys join him in mourning.

The city of Los Angeles is destroyed. This in and of itself is not unusual. The city of Los Angeles has been destroyed many times. He knows that from the movies. In 1953, Los Angeles was destroyed in a war of the worlds. In 1974, Los Angeles was destroyed in an earthquake. In 1984, Los Angeles was destroyed by a comet at night *and* the Terminator. The terminators came back in 1991 with a nuclear bomb. In 1996 came our Independence Day. 1991 was the year that the Soviet Union was destroyed. He knows it was destroyed because the new maps just call it Russia. Los Angeles is resilient. It comes back on the maps, year after year.

In all the movies Andreas has watched, though, he has never seen it get crushed. That usually happens to Tokyo.

Still, he mourns. The map used to be so big, but now, it is smushed, and all of the people—there used to be so many—are now smushed too. According to the 2010 census, Los Angeles has almost 4 million people—3,792,621 people, to be exact. He likes the census. Its website has a map. According to that website, Ridgecrest, California (although it is almost not California, considering how close it is to the Nevada border) only has 28,973 people. He is excited for the next census, although he wonders how many people will be born in 2020. In 2010, 97,257 (3,792,621 minus 3,695,364) people were born in Los Angeles. In 2010, 2,703 people were born in Ridgecrest. But he doesn't like the map on the census website. It has big, ugly dots in greens and blues all smushed on top of each other. That map is not smushed.

His map is, though. Smushed. Just like the city of Los Angeles. He wails.

"Andreas, stop it! Get out of your brother's room! We need to pick him up after his game today, and his room needs to be *clean!*" His mother grabs him, and he screams. He is still sad, but he's also screaming because she's grabbing him, her chipped fingernails like claws, squeezing his arm, making the skin *squish*, like the maps were squished, like the people on the maps were squished. He's hitting the floor in the hallway, the wood rock-hard, as unswayed as a fault line, without a carpet to cushion the blow, and he smushes his butt. It hurts now.

His ears hurt too. She is vacuuming. He holds his head and curls up in the hallway. He rocks and moans, the overhead fluorescent light in the hallway burning his eyes from behind the sockets, and the ceiling fan whirring like a drill whittling away at stone, but the light and the fan and vacuuming go on and on: a never-ending mining expedition to his ever-quickening racing heart.

At some point, the vacuuming, at least, stops. He peers back into his brother's room through the hallway door. His mother slams it open. She is standing in the doorway. She makes him look at her. There is an eyelash in her right eye.

She blinks rapidly to make it go away, but it stays like the dots on the census map.

"Say 'sorry,' Andreas," his mother orders him. "Repeat after me: 'Sorry.' 'Sorry.'"

He doesn't know what he's supposed to be apologizing for, and something on his face says that. The teachers tell him that his face can say a lot of things and so can other people's. He knows that. He can listen to other people's faces well enough. He just can't see his own face, so he can't listen to it.

His mother asks him to apologize again. Because he hit her. Andreas does not remember hitting her, but he is sorry. He knows hitting is bad, and he hates when he can't remember that he did something bad. The teachers say that knowing when you have made a mistake is half the battle. He knows he is losing that battle.

Andreas holds up his tablet so he can say sorry to her, but she gives him a withering glare. "You need to *say* sorry, Andreas. No typing!"

She makes to take his tablet away, and the boy hugs it against his chest, where his heart feels like it is going to burst like an earthquake, but she looks at the time and mutters something under her breath. "This conversation isn't over," she warns him.

His mother leaves the room, dragging the vacuum behind her. Andreas glares at it as it makes its escape. It is big and metal and gray, like a spaceship, retreating after the attack on Los Angeles in 1953. This spaceship sneaks under the radar because it, unlike the other spaceships, isn't green. Andreas winces with every thump it makes against the steps.

Andreas hates the vacuum even more than he hates the census website.

He retreats into his brother's room, but it's too late. His maps, painstakingly arranged on the floor, city maps on top of state maps, and state maps on top of the map of the nation, are gone without a trace.

He was going to show them to his brother.

The shadow of his mother stretches over him. "Stop crying about the maps! I've taken them away, so you don't need to worry about them anymore! It's time to go pick up your brother now. You need to look presentable. Come to the mirror with me! Can you say 'mirror'? 'Mir-ror…'"

Not just the city of Los Angeles is destroyed now. He has maps of California, maps of the Pacific Time Zone, maps of the United States, maps of North America, and maps of the world. Now that those maps are destroyed, their places are doomed too. Andreas scrambles to the window and waits for the sun to be blotted out by his mother's sneakers. The maps were stepped on. The world is underneath her feet.

CHAPTER 2

———

Andreas gasps as a snaggy knot causes his whole head to lurch. The woman rakes a hairbrush through the short, blond hair. As she tears at a final tangle, she puts her hands on her hips triumphantly. "There, that's better. Now you're presentable."

Andreas watches the brows furrow. He knows what mirrors are. But the person looking back at him isn't him. The person looking back at him is tall. They say five feet and three inches is tall for a twelve-year-old boy. But Andreas isn't tall. The way people look at him, he knows he must be small. They make him sit down and look them in the eye and hold it, like clenching your stomach to hold in the pee, and so all he ever wants to do is run to the bathroom to look at nothing. He likes to watch that false image swirl down the toilet.

The person looking back at him has short blond hair. He knows, from the movies, that blond hair is attractive. There is a lot of blond hair in California. The boys with the blond hair get the fuzzy lighting and the swelling music and the kisses. No one has ever kissed Andreas. He knows the blond boys in the movies get girls kissing them, but he will take anyone. His brother and mother don't count. When mothers kiss their kids, there isn't any fuzzy lighting or swelling music. Andreas isn't attractive. The person looking back at him in the mirror is wearing a zipper. Andreas doesn't wear zippers. Zippers pinch his skin, and the metal is cold, and sometimes, the sun hits the metal, and it goes into his eyes. The person in the mirror is who his mother wants him to be. It isn't difficult to figure out. Not when his mother says so. "Oh, how sweet! You look so handsome!"

So his mother thinks this imposter is handsome. Andreas looks at the mirror. The woman behind him has long, brown hair, burnt into curls. She has tan skin puckered with dark blotches: the lingering effects of sunburn. She has caked on so much dark makeup that it makes her swamp-colored eyes look like they're bulging hungrily. Andreas wonders what she sees when she looks at herself.

How can she be this excited for an image she constructed herself?

Andreas is not tall. Andreas is not attractive. Andreas does not wear zippers. Andreas is not like everyone else.

There is one thing that Andreas and the person in the mirror have in common. There is a scar across both of their right cheeks. He remembers this story. He dug his fingernails in, trying to dig out the pressure in his jaw from the clenching, from the screaming. Yes, he remembers. The reason why he was clenching was because Atlas, his cat, was hit by a car. He smiles at the memory of his cat.

He will always be sad that Atlas died. He will always be sad that Atlas was *murdered*, and no one went to jail, although it is the law that murderers go to jail, but the scar reminds him of Atlas before he died. Atlas would wake him up every morning by licking his right cheek. Atlas did that because he was hungry. If Andreas wouldn't wake up quickly enough,

Atlas would eat him! Atlas can't wake him up anymore, but he is still with him—always. His cheek can't get hit by a car.

He watches the person in the mirror smile back at him. He sticks his tongue out, a little to the left. He exhales the syllable: "heeeee." It's Andreas's smile.

His mother looks back in confusion, and the smile falls off her face. "I can't believe I almost forgot!"

She digs into her purse and smears the scar remover cream all over his cheek. The scar remover cream doesn't work, but the person in the mirror is unrecognizable regardless. Andreas would never hide the memento from Atlas.

* * *

They wait in the sun like cats, ready to capture something, in Ridgecrest High's parking lot. Andreas recognizes the others from their cars. Junior Jalen's guardians, Dominique and Riah, are in their white sedan. The whole Ortiz clan is coming to support their freshman, Gabriel, in their gray mini-van.

The other freshman on the team only has his father coming to support him, but Sadiq Senior is making up for it by transforming his plain, black car into a poster for school spirit on four wheels. Dion's parents' car trundles in despite the smushed front. The senior Eddie's red convertible will be missed next year—even though it's actually his older sister's car.

Ivory and his twin sister, Ebony, share their gray Mini-Cooper; sometimes, when she has one of her basketball games, he needs to catch a ride with one of his teammates. He most often rides with Marquis, who has a mini-van come pick him up, although only one person ever comes to the parking lot.

By contrast, the tiny car that comes to pick up Marcus is always stuffed to the brim with people. Bob and Tom's families have the exact same make and model of car; to differentiate them, they agreed to put their Ridgecrest High Soccer bumper stickers on opposite sides of their bumpers. And then there's player number eleven. He is the first one out of the bus. He's talking excitedly to Coach Diego, confident, despite how the coach is dwarfing his 5'5" height and slim build. Andreas can tell that his brother is happy because his hands are flapping, causing his long, brown hair to bounce. He's not trying to work out the snaggles with his fingers, and Coach Diego isn't making those green eyes look at him. Andreas watches his brother's hands. He sees the story his brother is telling: In the last thirty seconds of their game, York just *barely* blocked a final gambit from the opposing team. York says these things too, of course, but it's so much better with the hands making the ball out of the air. Coach Diego understands that.

Their mother doesn't. She runs up to the bus, making a bigger fuss than York ever did with her cries of "Calm hands! Calm hands!"

Andreas wonders how they are ever supposed to be normal, like she wants them to be, when she makes everything they do into a scene.

"Mom, Mom!" York exclaims, hands continuing to punctuate his joy. "Coach has been helping me, and we've been looking at the offer—"

"*What* offer?" she roars, although York has told her before, but she spent the entire time forcing him to look her in the eyes.

All ten sets of eyes from the other soccer players at Ridgecrest High are staring at them. They were ignoring York before. Their expressions are the same, but now York has to look at them. Andreas's cheeks burn for him.

"Heh, sorry," York hisses to his teammates. "Parents. You know?" They roll their eyes at him—although they really should be rolling their eyes at *Ms. Seaver*, Andreas thinks—careful to do so only behind Coach Diego. "Go, team!" York says to their retreating forms. "It's shaping up to be a great season for the Burros, huh?"

They don't answer. Andreas watches them go, filtering into their separate vehicles, dispersing like a coalition of cheetahs after the hunt is over, no respect paid to the one who won them their prize.

With a start, Andreas realizes that York's attention has shifted to him. "Hey, Skippy," he whispers. York's whispers aren't normal-person whispers. Normal people whisper because they don't want Andreas listening. York whispers because he wants Andreas to understand. "Too loud?"

It's *always* too loud. So nodding isn't lying. But it still feels wrong as they exit, and by the time the words line themselves up in his mind, and his fingers stop thrumming enough for him to input them on his tablet, the words, *"They don't like you,"* are entirely removed from their context. Normal people *never* like them, after all.

Andreas thinks it's because they go everywhere in disguise. There is nothing more untrustworthy than a cheaply-covered scar.

* * *

York's nose squishes when they enter his room. Their mother likes the smell. To be honest, Andreas does too: He likes the grounding punch of citrus scent. But he's never told her that.

York *has* told their mother that he doesn't like the smell of the air freshener. With words! She doesn't listen, not even when he bought an air freshener with a smell that he does like with Coach Diego. Their mother says it's because it's her house. Andreas knows that it's York's room.

York holds his nose as he creeps over to the windows, hoping to open them without betraying that to their mother. Andreas knows his brother doesn't like the smell, but if he opens the window, what if the maps fly out? Their mother couldn't have gotten rid of them for good, could she?

"No windows!" he tells his brother. *"Not yet!"* Turning at the sound of the tablet acting as his younger brother's voice, York swallows thickly but nods. *"Mom put away my maps,"* Andreas explains. Yes, they have to be out away, not destroyed. Or else he would know! He would have felt something!

His brother's non-pixelated voice reacts: "Oh, no!" Andreas would have used stronger words himself, but he knows that his mother hates swearing, although other twelve-year-old boys are allowed to swear. He thinks that his mother would hate if York swore, although York is nineteen, so he is legally an adult. When Andreas is legally an adult, he will move in with his brother.

York wraps a lock of his long, brown hair around his right index finger and spins it. When York was younger, he would spin his whole body, but he got in trouble for that. This spinning passes as more "normal."

Andreas thinks normal depends on the person, though. When York's facial hair first started growing in, he would touch it, but he said it was scratchy, so he has shaved regularly ever since. Andreas wants a beard, however. All the powerful sages in the movies stroke their beards. He knows from the movies that beards are manly. If he is manly enough, maybe someone will kiss him. He has never seen a woman with a beard get kissed, though. He wonders what kind of hair is "womanly."

What Andreas does know, though, is that he has never seen a beard-wise sage squeeze under a wooden frame.

His brother laughs from under his bed. Andreas looks quizzically. York crawls out with a glob of hair between his fingers.

"*Gross!*" Andreas yells at him.

"Aw, but you said you like my hair," York counters, frowning. That means he is sad.

They have had this conversation before. If he does not remember, *that* is sad. "*I like your hair on your head,*" Andreas informs him. "*Hair on the floor is gross. That is the rule.*"

"Well, if that's the rule…" But Andreas sees that York has placed it—hair, his own hair, fresh off the floor!—between his fingers and is rubbing it. Andreas does not say what he has seen, though, because he knows his brother is sad. York used to do the same thing to globs of fur from Atlas. York was always scared to touch the cat directly, but he *loved* Atlas' fur. Atlas had both black and white fur. York would swirl the black and white fur in his hands. York told him it was like paint, except that it didn't have that paint smell.

They agree that paint smells bad. That is normal.

York goes back under the bed while Andreas goes back to looking in the drawers. Things go back in the drawers; that is the rule. He looks back at his brother. York's green eyes shine back at him. Atlas had green eyes too. Andreas has to look away for a moment.

York knows he is still listening, though. "*Clothes* go in the drawer," he says. "That's the rule."

"*Well, if that's the rule…*" Andreas echoes, but he doesn't stop. His brother returns the favor: not saying anything.

They continue in comfortable silence—well, comfortable lack of conversation because York is humming to himself to stay focused—until Andreas hears a sharp cry of pain.

He whips around and hurries to the edge of the bed, where his brother is slithering out, groaning. With one hand, he gingerly rubs his head. With the other hand, he has a cluster of maps in his fist. Andreas gasps.

"Now don't be excited yet," York advises. "There's more."

As he goes back under the bed, Andreas scrambles down the spiraling metal stairs, down from the clustered bedrooms of the second floor to the cramped kitchen and living room of the first floor, to get the ice pack from the refrigerator. He almost trips up the stairs. It's fine, though.

By the time he returns, York has several crumpled piles in front of him and then smushes them all into his hands. Andreas tries not to wince at that. He extends the hand with the ice pack in it.

They do a trade. In comfortable lack of conversation, Andreas saves the world, smoothing the fault lines.

When the world is smooth, though, York rocks it with an earthquake of a question: "Hey, remember our deal?"

The thing about earthquakes is that they can start so small at first that you don't know what's going on. "*We didn't make a deal. Or else you would have broken it, by playing with floor-hair like that.*"

York chuckles. "We didn't shake on it, so it didn't happen!" He then shakes his head. "I was unclear. I apologize. It was a deal between me and Mom."

The floor caves from underneath him, and Andreas is suddenly thrust back on the ground floor of the house, abandoning his homework because he can hear York chasing his mother up the stairs.

* * *

He was doing math homework, Andreas remembers. Addition. Even though he was in middle school. As if you need to be able to talk to do math.

The kids in the regular classrooms talked all the time, their chatter scattering through the hallways because not only were they learning fine despite their chatter but their teachers hadn't learned to close the doors. Andreas was grateful, though, because he got to hear snippets of the lessons through those open doors.

Like, in the regular math classes, there are letters in math? What is that? He wanted to learn!

But he won't learn letter-math. Because the teachers can't fathom that he knows addition by now.

He had stopped doing his math homework in protest, but because they take away his tablet in class, he couldn't tell them what the protest was about.

So, they assumed it wasn't a protest. They assumed he couldn't do it.

That was when his mother decided that he needed to do his homework in the kitchen, where she could watch him. As if her breathing over his shoulder plus dinner-breath would equal him doing his homework. He protested.

She gave up. "I'm going upstairs! Don't bother following me until your homework's done!"

York, who was making a doodle, dithering around the dinner table, whipped his head up. "Mom! Wait, Mom! I want to tell you something!"

"Well, I want to get into my pajamas, so keep up, will you?"

After York scampered off, Andreas waited a few seconds before stuffing his homework into his folder and peering up the stairs. He knew that York didn't approve of him not doing his homework—that's against the rules—but York had never been forced to do the same math over and over for actual years.

"Mom, there's something I want to do."

"There are things we all want to do, sweetie, but they aren't necessarily things that we are able to do," she dismissed.

York held his ground. "Well, I've been talking to Coach Diego, and he thinks this is something I can do."

"What? Play on another soccer team?" their mother snorted. "I'm not going to ferry you from practice to practice!"

"What are you talking about, Mom? I drive myself to soccer stuff now!" Andreas heard his brother's nose whistle as he forced himself to take a deep breath. "I'm not talking about soccer, Mom. I'm talking about college."

Andreas heard their mother laugh. Laugh! "And what do you need to go to college for?"

"What does everyone else go to college for?"

"You're not getting into college."

"Well, not this very second, no—" York conceded, "—but, Mom, I'm a junior. I have a full year to get in!"

"Oh? And are you going to take the SAT, write an essay, and fill out applications for scholarships?" she challenged.

"Actually, I was thinking about taking the ACT. I've heard that the wording on the ACT is less…convoluted. Heh. That's an SAT word!"

Their mother made a claim, despite the evidence. "You're not willing to do the work."

"What if I am?"

"Then I guess you'll get in."

"And what'll happen if I get in?"

"You'll do something—that's as far as you've thought about it," she huffed.

"If I get into a college—any college—can I get your permission for something?" his brother broached.

"For what? Drinking? Getting a girlfriend? That's not something that's packaged in the college experience, you know."

York sputtered. "Getting drunk is against the law if you're under twenty-one!" He valiantly recovered. "I want to take Andreas on a road trip. He loves maps, and he has so many maps, but he's never been to any of those places—unless he has a map of Ridgecrest that I haven't seen. Actually—"

"Yeah. Sure. Whatever. I'm watching TV."

* * *

Andreas floats back up through the wooden boards, escaping the sounds of their mother's escapist television show. "How would you feel about going on a road trip with me and seeing the places on these maps?" York asks.

Andreas's joy cannot be contained by a sitting position! He must jump it out so the San Andreas Fault itself shudders at the vibrations.

York grins at his brother's excited skipping. "Okay, Skippy. I'll just remind Mom about our promise. Then, we can pack our stuff."

Andreas nuzzles York gratefully. The United States is so big that he'll get to be away from his mother for a long time. Does a better gift exist?

CHAPTER 3

———

At dinner, York broaches the subject. "So…" he says, twirling the spaghetti on his fork. "I got into college."

"So, you did," their mother mutters, snatching a napkin in her hand and smearing it across Andreas's face. "Andreas, there is tomato sauce on your face."

Andreas's face smushes. He knew that, and he was going to clean his face once the spaghetti strand was fully in his mouth! He pulls the remaining string of spaghetti out of his mouth, examining it to see if any napkin bits stuck on.

"And you said that when I got into college, I could take Andreas on a road trip." York looks at his brother and smiles.

Satisfied that his spaghetti does not have any napkin bits on it, Andreas sucks it into his mouth and hums contentedly.

Their mother dabs at her lips delicately. "And where would you take him, exactly?"

"To my college. It's in Albany, New York. You're from that state, aren't you, Mom?"

"Yes, to your question. But no to your request." She stands up and starts putting her cup and napkin into her empty bowl.

York's face reddens in warning colors. "What do you mean, *no*? You *promised* that we could go on the road trip when I got into a college!"

It wasn't a promise, Andreas recalls. It was a deal. Andreas is not surprised at their mother's rebuff. To her, all promises directed toward her are set in stone, but all promises she gives are, in fine print, negotiable, and their reading comprehension never quite reaches a *proficient* level, as the speech therapist at school would say.

At the playground, when someone gets too close, she says, "I'm sorry, my son can't talk." Andreas never even got the chance to comment on the girl's t-shirt depicting the two titanic beasts facing off: "Hey! Do you think they'll make King Kong and Godzilla friends next movie?"

At the after-school meetings, when an invitation to a social gathering for "kids like him" is issued, she says, "I'm sorry, my son can't come." Andreas never had the opportunity to ask, "Will I know anyone there?"

At the grocery store, when he accidentally knocks something over, she says, "I'm sorry, my son can't understand." Andreas didn't have to ask, "How do I help fix it?" It's the same grocery store they've been to all his life. He knows how the shelves are organized. He even recognizes the employee who comes over to re-stack the cans. Barry has been working at Wal-Mart for over twenty years. Andreas started putting them back, but his mother pulled him away. As if Barry, for all the years he's been working at the same Wal-Mart, didn't know who they were. As if the parents of the same people he and York have gone to elementary, middle, and high school with don't know who *they* are. They know them well enough to decide that they don't like them. Because they don't know him at all, except as "can't talk, can't come, and can't understand."

So many things he *can't* do. He's not angry about it. Not anymore. When he's a legal adult, he'll move out. He'll be eighteen. Parents don't have control over eighteen-year-olds. That's the law.

York is still getting used to the new law. He has told him that he doesn't feel like an adult yet.

Maybe York will feel more like an adult when Andreas moves in with him. Why can't he be eighteen *now?*

Maybe if he were an adult, their mother would listen to him. Andreas hears tears clog his brother's throat. York is sad—no, more than sad. He's feeling *betrayed.* That means he was getting ready to be happy…when that opportunity was snatched out from under him. Taking Andreas on a road trip would have made York happy. Andreas swallows the bubbly feeling that thought gives him.

"No, I am not letting you drag that boy across the country! Can you imagine how *traumatizing* that would be for him?" She dumps her bowl, napkin, and cup into the sink. Andreas and York both wince at the noise.

Regardless of the noise, Andreas can imagine how *amazing* it would be. He's reassembled the United States, state by state, fifty times over. (He's since upgraded to a greater challenge: re-building states county by county. Many states are just wannabe squares, after all.)

And without his mother around, he can let his actions say who he is. He's not normal, but he's still okay. York said so, and York is the one he will be going on the trip with.

Andreas remembers when he punched York. That was not okay. It didn't matter that Atlas was murdered, and no one went to jail, although it is the law that murderers go to jail. It is never okay to hit. It is never okay to hit your brother.

* * *

But York, even as his eye swelled, even as Andreas felt good that someone else, someone else who people listened to, had a physical token of the pain inside of him that demanded to be looked upon and talked about, told him that he was okay. "It's okay. I'm okay. You're okay. Let it out. Let it go. It's okay to feel not okay."

Andreas thought that their mother wasn't listening to that, as she tore them apart and wrapped up Atlas' body in a big black trash bag and threw him away.

It's okay to feel nervous about meeting someone new. It's okay to be tired after a long day talking. It's okay to feel embarrassed around people. Andreas feels those ways all the time.

But that's okay.

When Andreas asked York that night, under a navy star-spangled banner, if he felt okay about him, York answered, "Always."

York gave him another essence of permanence that night too. "See the brightest thing in the sky this night? It's not actually a star! It's a planet! Venus!" Venus was as bright as a cat's eye, and under its light, the cut on his cheek burned. By morning, it was clear that it, too, would be permanent.

Their mother talked about heaven like it was someplace high in the sky that they'd never see. Andreas wondered why she doesn't look up. Doesn't she know that it's okay to feel lonely at night?

* * *

Andreas thinks their mother doesn't know what's okay. She doesn't know that breaking a promise is against the rules. He's not angry, though. Because they'll prove her wrong.

They *can* talk. They *can* come. They *can* understand.

They *will* travel.

Andreas tugs at York's shirt sleeve. He sees his brother rub tears away from his eyes—York had not allowed himself that display of vulnerability before their mother stomped off to her room—before the teen says to him, "What is it?"

What this is is stupid, is what Andreas wants to say, but he knows that he needs to work up to that. *"Let's go to your room,"* is what he says through his tablet in the meantime.

As the boys enter York's room, York is still working on drying his eyes. Which is fine. It will take Andreas a while to take out his maps anyway. He takes his collection of crazy-shaped counties. They look silly to him. They should look silly to York.

But York is just staring at the picture blankly. *"St. Martin Parish,"* Andreas explains.

"Are...are we playing a guessing game?" York asks. Andreas supposes that maybe they are. Although what Andreas is guessing is how many counties he'll have to go through before his brother's eyes are dry.

"What state?"

York hums…"You said 'parish,' right? You've told me that a few states have weird names for things."

Andreas nods. *"Louisiana and…"* he prompts.

"New York?" York guesses.

"New York's boroughs are parts of New York City. If we're talking about states that have weird names for counties—" All states have weird names for "things." *"—the other state that*

doesn't call counties "counties" is Alaska. Alaska's counties are called boroughs."

Andreas pulls out his Alaska packet. *"Alaska's counties are also huge,"* he explains. *"Because Alaska is huge."*

York flips through the packet and sighs. "Too bad we can't go there."

"We can't go to Alaska," Andreas concedes. *"Because Canada is in the way—"* And Canada is even bigger than Alaska! *"—but we still have forty-eight states that don't have Canada or the Pacific Ocean in the way."*

York looks scandalized. "But Mom said..."

Andreas exits out of the internet browser tab of the map of North America—because he doesn't have a map of Canada to show how it separates Alaska from the lower forty-eight states—and turns the volume on his tablet to its maximum. He doesn't care if she hears because he's heard her say it. *"Mom said you wouldn't get into a college."*

York's eyes bulge. "Turn the volume down!" he hisses. Andreas stares at him, unmoved. So York pleads, "But I *did* get into a college."

"You did," the tablet booms. Only now does Andreas return the volume to its normal level. *"So, you can do this too."* Andreas pulls his box of maps between them. *"We have the maps we need!"*

"It's not just about maps—" York protests.

"You have a car," Andreas points out. *"Mom said you wouldn't learn how to drive."*

"Mom says a lot of things—"

"Mom said I couldn't get the kitten to come inside. Atlas slept in my bed that first night." Andreas smiles at the memory and instinctively rubs at the cheaply-covered scar on his

cheek, in the place where Atlas would lick his face to wake him up in the morning. *"Mom is* wrong *about a lot of things."*

They *can* talk. They *can* come. They *can* understand.

They *will* travel. And she will have to have "Calm hands! Calm hands!" about it.

Because Andreas knows that their mother is wrong about the most important thing: Disguises don't *work.* Their mother's wish for York is for him to never reach too far because his disguise, his own cheaply-covered scar, could tear.

The disguise is already in tatters. They're not like everyone else. No one else's mother says their child "can't talk, can't come, and can't understand." No one else's mother cries "Calm hands! Calm hands!"

York looks furtively at his room's closed door. "You don't think she'll be mad?" he whispers.

"Oh, she'll be mad, but—she won't stop us," Andreas reassures his brother. Because stopping them would expose how wrong she is. If she just sits down in her room, her TV blaring, then she can pretend that she's still right.

"Okay," York takes a shuddering breath. "Okay. Let's pack our things."

It's easy to step out of the scraps, especially under the nocturnal vigil of cat's eye Venus.

CHAPTER 4

———

There is something soothing about the gas station at dawn. Not the smells, of course. Oil and exhaust and sweaty man sweat are gross. Gandalf probably had sweaty man sweat, but he was cool; he had a beard *and* the ability to lead *and* the power to magically clean himself. Andreas wishes he had magic. Oil and exhaust and sweaty man sweat are gross, though—that's the rule. Still, there is something soothing about the gas station at dawn.

The sights are not what's soothing, of course. Pulling into a lone building in the middle of a desert, to be honest, is unnerving. Andreas thinks it might be the sounds: the rolling of tumbleweeds, the reedy playback on the radio, and, most of all, calm silence, in the absence of people. It's unnerving to pull into a lone building in the middle of a desert, but it's a relief to declare yourself king of the castle.

And EddieWorld on I-15 N is a magnificent castle. It makes so much sense to make your building shaped like a bowl of ice cream to advertise ice cream. Why don't more ice cream parlors do that? Andreas has great respect for "Eddie"—who must be the man wearing red depicted on the front of the building. He wonders why he didn't do the next logical step, though: making the gas station section of his world gas-station-shaped.

"Ooh, Skippy!" his brother exclaims. "They make home-made ice cream here!"

Andreas looks at the time on his tablet, and his brow furrows. *"It's 6:30 a.m.,"* he informs him.

"So?" York prompts.

Andreas cannot believe he is having this conversation. Ridgecrest is only an hour and a half away. They cannot return within the day with their stomachs cramped and their poop runny. *"So, you have a sensitive stomach. Ice cream is not a breakfast. That's the rule."*

"Well, if that's the rule…"

Andreas sighs as York slides out of the car and traipses toward the ice cream castle. Andreas hopes Eddie will turn his foolish brother around.

He unbuckles his seatbelt to access the box of Cheerios stowed away behind his seat. As he climbs over the console to eat the cereal in the back—He doesn't want crumbs where he's sitting!—he spots another car pull in.

The other car is, in fact, a truck. The truck is red, but the paint is chipped. It matches the pump the truck pulls up next to.

Which is the pump right next to them.

If the man with the sunburnt left arm wants to blow himself up with his cigarette while re-filling his gas, he can at least choose to do so in private. As it is, however, Andreas does not want to be blown up. He pokes his head out of the window, pulling up a graphic, a picture of a real fire from a real gas station caused by a real cigarette, explaining the risk—he knows that while sometimes he can't understand a thing that people's words are telling him, pictures help him make sense of the world. The cigarette-blowing-up man looks at the graphic, rubs at his baggy eyes, then mutters something to himself. He kicks at an idle plastic bag. When he hits the bag, it hisses, and the man swears and drops his cigarette. Not close enough to the gas pump, thank goodness. "What was that?" the man barks.

Privately, Andreas is thankful to the do-gooder bag, which distracted the cigarette-blowing-up man by hissing at him. Andreas knows he is right to spotlight the risk, but at the same time, he knows that when people don't want the spotlight on them, they can do very bad things. Wrong things. Like attacking a bag that isn't doing anything to them.

He leans down, searching for the Cheerios box, hoping he didn't spill it. York has warned him that a mess will inevitably come from spending weeks in the car, but Andreas wants the car to be as clean as possible for as long as possible.

Besides, if *he* is the one to make the first mess, York will laugh. It will not be a mean laugh, but it will remind him of mean laughs. So many things he can't do. Like keep himself clean.

A yowl cuts through the early morning: a call to action. Andreas presses himself against the window.

Crawling out of the bag is a cat. The cat is rearing back, the hair on her back puffed and taut. The cat is curling her tail around her side protectively, but even so, she is starting to crouch toward the ground, not sure what to do but acutely aware that she can no longer stay in her shelter.

Andreas does not need to be normal to know that the cat has been hit. Hitting is wrong. He really does not need to be normal because the culprit, as dismissive of lives blown up because of cigarettes at gas stations as the life of the cat he has kicked, admits to the crime: "Scram, you filthy animal, or I'll do it again!"

No one is around. What do they tell him at school? *"See something? Say something!"* He remembers how the neighbors all stood and stared. They all saw Atlas get murdered. They all saw the murderer career away. None of them said anything.

The cat is the color of Atlas' fur swirled. The man's shadow is as large and inevitable as the car's.

Andreas refuses to be helpless. Not again.

He jams his finger on his tablet's volume buttons. *"STOP!"*

The man swerves around. "The what—?" he grunts, ape-like.

"STOP HITTING!" His tablet is his monster's roar. Andreas pushes the car door open. York left the keys inside. He wouldn't leave his brother without air conditioning—and Andreas wouldn't allow it, knowing how noncommittal he can be about food.

Just like Andreas isn't going to allow this. It doesn't matter how large and inevitable the man is. If he thinks he can attack a defenseless creature, he will learn how large and inevitable and—what's the word his mother calls him?—*unpredictable* he can be.

"Who are you? Some kind of idiot? Get out of here, kid. Go back to your mommy." The thing is that is exactly the type of thing his mother would say. More saccharine, of course. This is more understandable. The boy is thankful for it.

"Stop hitting the cat."

"I'll do what I damn well please." The man considers. "Hey, was that you eyeballing me at the pump too? Pay for your own gas. Unless…your mommy can't afford it. Tell her that this is a free country. We don't give handouts."

Andreas has money! He could pay for the gas if he wanted to! It's just that…he can't even drive! That's against the law!

He will drive, when he's eighteen, and moved out of his mother's house, but, right now, he's paying for things like his cereal—a sensible breakfast—and *not* ice cream at 6:30 a.m.

And…a free country? There is no country where you are free to kick at things that make you mad. This man makes no sense! *"Hitting the cat is wrong,"* Andreas informs him.

"I'd steer clear of telling me what to do until you can actually *say* it." Between one second and the next, the tablet is snatched from Andreas's hands. Andreas yelps. "She can afford this but not gas. We're becoming a welfare state, I tell you. That's lucky for you, you know that? In the good old days, we'd make sure people like you knew how to fend for themselves."

At first, Andreas had yelped in fear. Now, he is seething with anger. How dare this person proclaim him *lucky?* He is not *lucky* to have a tablet. He is lucky to have a *voice.* And that voice was not bestowed upon him by some spirit of fortune, but the whims of a father he does not remember ever seeing in person, a father who thought, "Wouldn't it be funny if a six-year-old had a brand-new tablet for his birthday?"

Brand-new at the time. What exactly does this man hope to gain by taking it from him? There's only one thing he can possibly be getting. The boy thinks enough people have power over him.

Andreas knows it is wrong to hit, but he also knows that it is wrong to steal. The sunburnt man did two wrong things. Andreas will only be doing one wrong thing, and the math rules say…

"I'm so sorry!" York cries from behind him. Andreas does not turn around, although his eye twitches as the sunburnt man looks upon his brother like he is something to be pitied. No, something to make *submit* to him. "My brother doesn't understand!"

Andreas whips around. He blinks rapidly, but his eyes are burning. They're burning with betrayal. He was prepared to feel happy that his brother would support him, but now... He is making the sunburnt man happy.

The sunburnt man crosses his arms smugly. He has found someone who will submit. "So, your mommy's not around."

York shoots a confused glance at him, but Andreas turns away and climbs back into the car.

He hears the sunburnt man coo something about how ungrateful children are and how good he is to forgive them. Andreas thinks about how good it would feel to punch him.

But he doesn't. Because that's what they predict when they call him *unpredictable*. Andreas stalks off to the car, slamming the passenger-side door shut.

The driver-side door to the car creaks. Andreas jolts. York is looking at him. York's hands are empty. Except for the tablet. Andreas takes it, but his brother's hands are now pointing outside.

Andreas's brow furrows. *"I thought you got ice cream?"* he asks tentatively.

"I gave it to him. Payment for your tablet."

Andreas looks away, cursing the fluttering in his chest that he recognizes as *some* sort of emotion. It doesn't matter that York got his tablet back. It was wrong that it was taken from him in the first place!

"Come on," York urges. "I think the cat is still around."

He isn't going to be distracted that easily. *"Why did you do it?"* he demands.

"Because he doesn't matter. What matters are the ones he was going to hurt: the cat...and you. It felt gross to suck up to him, but I'd rather be nursing my pride than nursing someone back to health." He laughs, but there's no joy in it. "I've gotten pretty good at the former, but…" He cuts himself off. "I never want the opportunity to get good at the latter."

How wrong is the world to force that choice? Still, Andreas's choice is clear. He pushes his head into his brother's stomach, stretching across the console.

"Thanks for forgiving me," York murmurs, as if in shock of the accepting headbutt.

It's not forgiveness. It's being bigger, being better, smushing those feelings of betrayal down to put up a comforting face toward what matters.

"*Let's help that cat,*" Andreas tells him, his chest burning with determination.

CHAPTER 5

———

The cat is afraid of him. Andreas feels like he has been forcibly enlarged. He's the irradiated monster just trying to get back to the sea. But they're at the edge of the Mojave Desert. There's no sea to be seen.

The cat is not afraid of York, though. York did not yell. York did not hit. (York did not want to hit.) York, though, is nervous around her. That isn't going to work. His fingers spasm as he tries to touch the feline's fur.

Andreas pads back to the car. He climbs into the back seat and reaches over the headrest. His blanket—olive green, frayed at the edges, stained with rivers of tears—is lying on top of his suitcase. He gathers it into his hands. It's the only thing that seems to fit his hands. But it will also fit around the cat. As he approaches his brother, he clears his throat—so York and the cat will not be startled.

"Skippy?" York whispers reverently. "You can't mean…"

But Andreas shakes his head and points to the cat, who is still shaking from her ordeal. Her yellow eyes stare at York beseechingly. The collar around her neck is the same color. *She is what matters*, Andreas reminds himself, straining not to think of a black-and-white-cat with green eyes and a collar of the same color.

Andreas lies down and clicks his tongue. The cat creeps toward him. Just as she gets into range, he makes his move, swaddling her in the olive green blanket. She thrashes and screams, but the fight leaves her as she is soothed by the blanket, overriding how betrayed she feels by her own body. Andreas looks to his brother, who accepts the bundle of cat and blanket.

"It feels good, doesn't it?" Andreas asks her.

Her yellow eyes open and close slowly. Relief. Andreas smiles. He feels his tongue poke out of his mouth. Then, he starts to hop in place.

"Sure does, Skippy."

Andreas stops hopping because York doesn't deserve to feel all good after what he did today.

They take the bundle of cat and close all the windows before they start up the car, just in case she is frightened by its noise. York passes the bundle to Andreas so he can drive. In that moment, he seems to register it for the first time. "What are we doing?"

"Getting her home," the boy answers definitively. *"She has a collar. She must have one."*

The young man peers out the window. They are once again alone at EddieWorld. "I don't think it's here."

Andreas nods in agreement. He reaches under his seat, where he has stowed away the packet of California maps. He has forty-nine packets just like it. York has told him that they won't be visiting all fifty states—not enough time— but Andreas is prepared. And hopeful that his brother will change his mind.

The first page of the packet is a general state map. Since they are on a major road, it does not take Andreas long to pinpoint their location and mentally backtrack to the last town. He inputs Barstow in the car's GPS. (Andreas doesn't trust the GPS—it doesn't have the years of quality assurance of maps—but as long as he is allowed to grade and correct it, their relationship will be a cordial one.)

"What if we don't find her home in town?" his older brother presses. "We can't keep her. Cats don't belong in cars."

Andreas looks down at the blanket in his lap. The gray cat is now tentatively sniffing his hand. He allows her to before testing...Ah, yes, Atlas loved being scratched between the ears too.

But this isn't Atlas, and he will not be the one who drives away after taking someone else's Atlas away.

Then we will drop her off at a shelter. Someone is looking for her.

When the car starts up, the cat jolts, but Andreas calms her down by bunching the blanket around her tighter. She relaxes as her thrumming body is enveloped in a warm, constant swaddle.

* * *

"...This is distracted driving," York breathes.

Andreas allows a long sigh to escape him. The gray cat pokes her head out from where she has been scratching the middle seat and meows inquiringly. Distracted driving is texting or calling while driving. They're hardly texting or calling a cat. And they're not drinking or doing drugs either! It's perfectly legal to have a cat. It's perfectly legal to have a car. Therefore, it's perfectly legal to have a cat in a car!

Andreas thinks his brother would be less distracted if he looked only at the road. He's perfectly capable of looking for signs on both sides so York can do the *oh-so-difficult* job of staring straight ahead! Engaging in the conversation, though, will only make York more distracted, so Andreas helps him by looking back at his tablet. The Barstow Humane Society website *looks* like someone's school project, but, lo and behold, it is a 501(c)3 organization. Whatever that means.

Is it downloading an audio file? Why is it downloading an audio file? The audio file causes the internet browser on the old tablet to crash. He sticks to the search engine to look for its address.

"*2480 E. Main Street,*" Andreas tells his brother so York can input it in the GPS that he inexplicably trusts more than him.

"E. Main Street?" York chirps. "What's that?"

Andreas shrugs. Why doesn't he ask the GPS? *It* seems to know. Andreas's map, at least, confirms its existence. That's enough for him. The GPS tells him it's a twenty-minute drive. Andreas assures his brother that he can drive for twenty minutes.

"If I can drive this heavy machinery for twenty minutes, you can hold the fluffy cat for twenty minutes," York counters. That is a good argument.

What's a better argument is that this cat really loves being petted. Just like Atlas did.

* * *

As they turn off I-15 S, E. Main Street immediately demands their attention. Well, half of it does. Half of it is a line of restaurants, but it's just facing the desert, punctuated with billboards—coincidentally, also focused on food. One is about how you should not eat meat. It's next to a steakhouse. Oops. York's stomach growls as they pass a Starbucks.

"What would you even do there?" Andreas asks. *"Get some cookies?"*

Andreas knows Starbucks has real breakfast options: things like cereal and bagels. Plenty of non-meat things, to make the billboard happy! York knows this too, but Andreas knows that his brother would choose to eat the chocolate chip cookies. Even as he chastises him, though, he is looking for sources of breakfast. Was it IHOP that York got sick at? No, it was Denny's! Andreas doesn't trust either of them, but if he doesn't get some breakfast in his brother soon, he really will just grab some cookies.

As they pass the Starbucks, there is a bit of congestion in front of the Barstow Mall: the highest concentration of stores. As they wait, Andreas finds himself searching for a better restaurant within the complex. He doesn't find that.

He finds something better.

He squeaks in excitement and starts frantically punching in the address.

"What? What?" York yelps. "I can't stop! This is a *street!*" So, York keeps driving.

As the GPS refreshes, Andreas explains, *"I just saw a lost cat poster."*

"Make a U-turn," the GPS advises.

"U-turn?" York whimpers. "Where, though?"

Is his brother seriously asking that question? The desert is there for the U-turning! As York pulls over on a dusty bank—one that is a little too close to the vegan billboard for his liking—in order to begin his U-turn, Andreas prepares him to look for the poster. *"Stop. On your..."* Andreas needs a moment to calculate. *"...left."*

York gasps as he sees it: a gray cat sitting on the lap of an elderly woman, the picture pinned to a sign across the street. Andreas smiles at the feline. *You're going home!* The cat looks as calm as ever. Andreas admires her control over her facial expressions.

* * *

The car rumbles off the road and into a dusty, smushed trailer park—like maps crammed under a bed. York's green eyes flit around. "Are you sure this is the place?" he asks.

The cat answers his question. Her eyes narrow. Andreas discerns that she is disappointed in his brother's lack of faith. For his part, the boy gestures at her, in all her wise judgment. "Okay, okay," York relents. "Do we just go around knocking on each of these trailers until someone claims her?"

"Or we can announce that we're here, with the gray cat from the lost cat posters," Andreas suggests.

"Ooh, I like that idea better! Less disturbing people who don't want to be disturbed!" Andreas considers pointing out that shouting can disturb people who don't want to be disturbed, but he decides that losing your cat is more disturbing than hearing a stranger shouting. People shout all the time, and if they don't want to hear the shouting, they can use earplugs—or headphones, if you don't trust that the earplugs will come out of your ears.

"Hellooo!" York hollers. "We have the cat from the lost cat poster near Barstow Mall!"

The door to the trailer immediately across from them slams open. A short, elderly woman in a faded red dress echoes, "Stormy! Where are you?"

Inside the car, the cat, apparently named Stormy, hops out of the swaddle and paws at the grizzled, sun-worn hand that is blowing kisses at her through the window.

"Hello, Stormy!" the owner of the hand coos.

Laughter bubbles out of Andreas: a prolonged "hee" coupled with snorting. For his part, York just looks relieved. Andreas opens the door. Stormy launches herself onto an anthill immediately. It is smushed.

The woman guffaws. "Fun's over, Stormy!" she exclaims. She looks at York and Andreas. "Where did you find her?"

"At a gas station," York answers.

"A gas station!" she echoes. "Stormy, what in the world were you doing at a gas station? Are there not enough anthills to torment here?"

The cat turns her head in a rebuke, but when she opens the door to her trailer, the feline bounds into it, darting between her legs. The woman clicks her tongue reproachingly, but she also laughs, so she clearly is not actually angry. Andreas understands. It's hard to get angry at a cat. It's impossible to *stay* angry at a cat.

Then, strangely, the woman turns around. "Aren't you coming in, boys?"

York sputters. Andreas looks quizzically at him. He knows the lesson: stranger danger. But this woman isn't a threat to them. It has not escaped Andreas's notice how she stops to breathe after every sentence and how tightly she grips the railing as she ascends the three steps up to her trailer. If anything, they are a threat to *her* since they can breathe quietly and go up stairs without holding onto railings.

Sensing confusion between them, at the top of the steps, the woman turns around. "I can't really offer you any money." Andreas furrows his brow. He doesn't recall money being offered on the lost cat poster. The woman coughs, but when York winces, she waves it away. "Honestly, my tapsilog is probably worth more than any money I can give you."

"*Tapsilog?*" It is now Andreas's turn to wince. The tablet has surely butchered that name.

Instead of glowering at the desecration, though, the woman grins with honest, yellowing teeth. "Breakfast! From my homeland."

The boy looks at his brother knowingly. York tries to look innocent, but his stomach betrays him.

The woman laughs. "It'll be good tapsilog, I promise! I didn't feed my husband for thirty years…" She stops to take a breath. "…without getting *some* skill in it!" Her wrinkles twist into silent stories as she laughs. Andreas senses that she's laughing at the husband more than herself, although he doesn't appear to be around. "Now whether you'll like tapsilog? I don't take responsibility for that."

Andreas looks at his brother. Tapsilog doesn't seem like a dessert. In fact, it seems like a sensible breakfast. This is a sign to stay away from the chocolate chip cookies!

York chuckles. "Okay, we'll come in. Thank you for your generosity."

And that is when York's phone rings. He looks down at it and goes pale. When Andreas tries to look at the number that is causing him so much distress, though, York stows the phone away in his pocket. "You go on ahead," he says, waving him away. "I'll be right behind you. I just have to answer this. Go on, be polite to make up for my rudeness."

Andreas looks between his brother and the woman worriedly. Stormy plops down on the bottom stair. "*No!*" Andreas tells her. "*We're eating inside!*" He ushers the cat back up the stairs and follows behind her as she curls up on a low table between two old, scratched-up sofas.

"Stormy!" her owner scolds, but cats are famously impossible to move by words alone if they do not want to move. The old woman shakes her head. "Oh, well. We can use the big plates as a replacement for the table." She takes out an opened plastic bag of paper plates, takes out two, and starts pouring something on them. Andreas gets up to observe.

While the name tapsilog is unfamiliar to him, he recognizes the components of the dish: beef, fried rice, and a sunny-side-up egg. Andreas likes beef and rice. He only likes eggs hard-boiled, though. When the woman notices him watching and asks, "Like what you see?" though, he nods. Two out of three is the majority, after all.

The duo plop down on the sofas opposite of each other. Both are experienced enough with cats not to attempt to wait for Stormy to move off the table.

As Andreas eats the tapsilog, pushing apart the beef, the fried rice, and the egg on his paper plate, though, Andreas doesn't care how *rude* he is being as he sits on the woman's couch, peering out the window, resting his plate against the couch's top, watching his brother go from nervous to a submissive blank slate. What kind of rude thing has their mother shoved down York's throat? Andreas swallows thickly. Whatever it is, it's ruining *his* appetite too.

CHAPTER 6

———

Andreas hears a chirp next to him. He startles. It's Stormy, sharpening her claws on the top of the sofa. The boy scratches the cat's head, and she purrs.

He hears a chuckle behind him. "She likes you. Have you had a cat before?"

Andreas is jolted out of a memory of Atlas scratching at his bedpost. Something of the experience must have bled onto his face because Stormy's owner shakes her head. "Sorry. I'm being pushy. I was pushy to ask you two to come inside in the first place. You clearly have somewhere to be."

Andreas starts typing at his tablet—No, it's not her fault!— but his hostess is already packing some tapsilog into plastic bags. "For the road," she says as she hands the food to him.

"*Thank you,*" Andreas tells her.

He wants to tell her so much more. *It's not your fault. Why did you choose to trust us? Do you have kids? Do you have room in your heart for more kids?* But that's silly. That last one, anyway. Andreas has a mother, and, furthermore, he has a place for his heart.

That place is with his brother.

Andreas's mother knows where his heart is too. She must. Or else how would she know how to break it so efficiently?

When Andreas trots outside, York hastily puts away his phone. "Sorry, Skippy. You know how Mom can be."

Andreas knows how their mother *can* be, but he needs to know how she *was*. *"What did she say?"*

"You know—" York dismisses. "—she was surprised."

There are good surprises and bad surprises. A good surprise is getting to go on a road trip with his brother. A bad surprise is their mother calling them during that road trip. In other words, York is refusing to answer his question.

Andreas climbs into the car and buckles his seatbelt. When he hears the *click* of the seatbelt next to him, he asks again, *"What did Mom say to you?"*

"I mean, she said she was surprised to wake in the morning and see that we were gone! I feel bad. Maybe we should have told her?"

Ah. That is what their mother told him: to feel bad. Luckily, Andreas is not as vulnerable to inappropriate guilt as York. *"You did tell her, though,"* he points out. *"You said that when you got into college, you would be going on a road trip."*

"Yeah, but she didn't believe that would happen—"

"So?" Andreas challenges. *"That sounds like* her *problem, not ours."*

York's face goes red. "When you put it that way…But she wasn't just talking about herself. She…also made some good points about you." A chill races up Andreas's spine, and he sucks in a breath to keep from freezing on the spot. "She said that you didn't expect me to get into college either, that you miss home and your things, that you've never even left the state before, so you must be scared—"

When Andreas lets go of the breath he was holding, it's like fire. His throat burns from the screaming. York stares at him, wide-eyed. The boy punches out the words on his tablet. *"Why does* Mom *get to tell* you *how* I *feel?"*

"I didn't expect to get into college! I miss…some things… about home, and I'm a little bit scared about going to places I've never been before!"

"But did I *say any of those things?* I *can say so little. Don't put words in my mouth."*

York's face falls. "I made a mistake," York admits. "When Mom was saying those things, she said them about you, but maybe she said they were about you because you weren't there. Or maybe she just said things about me and said they were about you, so I could feel like I had something to protect."

"You do *have something to protect,"* Andreas insists. *"This deal. The next time she tries to guilt you out of this, remember that you're just upholding your end of the deal: a deal she freely made."* Before he can think better of it, he adds another important detail. *"Besides, when the deal is done, you won't be the one facing her surprise."*

As a thick haze of silence casts a pall over them, Andreas offers the most important piece of information of all: *"For the record, I always believed you'd get in."* Wasn't it obvious that he would?

* * *

Las Vegas is a city of believers: believers in money. Andreas believes in money, so why *not* go?

York wasn't sold on the idea. "Are you watching the same movies as me? They always lose money!"

"So?" the little brother challenged. "*They always end up winning in the end!*" And, yes, sometimes, it's not money, but Andreas will take fuzzy lighting and swelling music too. Their mother didn't believe that York would get into college, but he did, so why can't that happen, despite the disbelief?

That is how they end up including Las Vegas, Nevada on their agenda.

The first thing the brothers register is the lighting and the music. Whereas the movies calibrate it so the hero's musings about wealth and corruption can be heard, neither Andreas nor York can hear themselves talk, never mind *grumble*, as the hero so often does, as they drive down The Strip: a blaring beacon of the belief in glitz and glamor, yet, just beyond the monument to money is the utterly free desert.

The Strip is a section of land that technically does not belong to Las Vegas. It is "unincorporated." It does not pay Las Vegas. The map calls it Paradise. Andreas calls it Hell.

What other place than Hell could have lights that make his mouth dry, music that makes his ribcage rumble, and people who smell—not even like people but *things*. Things that make people crash into each other like waves and make words froth out as incomprehensible bubbles.

Truly that is the sin of this city.

Still, they have made plans for the city: Andreas really wants to see a tiger. He knows that they have tigers in Las Vegas! He's watched tigers get put in suitcases! In the movies *and* in the news!

As long as they're *baby* tigers, what he's also seen on the news won't happen to him.

Andreas blinks as he hears the car stop and does not resist as his brother reaches for his hand as they get out. They need to claim each other, in this place claimed by no one. That doesn't mean that the feeling of slick hands rubbing against each other doesn't cause him to sink deeper into Hell, where sight and sound and touch and taste and smell are all a single inferno.

The one good thing about Hell is that no one talks to him. One of the many bad things about Hell is that it seems like everyone wants to talk to York. They want to read his fortune or sell him a good luck charm or urge him to "become a man" at one of the casinos.

York isn't allowed in any of the casinos, never mind Andreas. The law is that you need to be twenty-one to enter the casinos.

Andreas checks his facts on his tablet. Oh. You can enter the casinos at any age, but you need to be at least twenty-one to do anything casino-y.

"You know, I thought I would be upset that we aren't allowed *inside* any of these places," York admits as he watches a couple stumble out from one of the casinos, limbs wobbly, the same wobbly when you look at something underwater from above the water. "But now I'm thinking that this is a good thing: The desert is right here."

It is the Mojave Desert: that furnace casting the blazing lights and sound in an otherworldly haze. The Mojave Desert is the driest desert in North America. Normally, Andreas would pity the person stuck measuring such things, but, today, the vast stretches of nothing is an ambrosia. The desert is powerful. The desert is the devil that the city dances with, says all of the climate experts, but Andreas cannot see it as the enemy of this story. No, he's sure of it now. The oasis truly is in the desert. It is the civilization on the horizon that is the mirage.

"Isn't very *fabulous*, is it?" Andreas cocks his head at York in confusion. York takes that as an indication to demonstrate, crooning the song with the very misleading title, "Welcome to Fabulous Las Vegas," by Brandon Flowers. York gets up and begins to spin in place, splaying his arms out in a carefree twirl. Except it isn't. Andreas knows his brother well enough to know that York is spinning the too-much away. Dizziness is one thing to focus on. It's also something that he has the power to create.

Andreas knows that his brother is serenading the desert. The woman who comes up behind them as they pass a casino does not. "Hi…" she murmurs. She is in a skin-tight black dress and red high heels.

York jolts. "Oh, hello! Do you also like the desert?"

She misses the obvious cue. "You have a *fabulous* singing voice." She reaches out to run a finger along York's jawline.

Whatever embarrassed blush could have come is chased away by a nervous sweat. "No…It's nothing, really. I've just listened to that song a million times." York looks to his brother for help.

Andreas has, unfortunately, also listened to The Killers a million times, whether they're in the form of The Killers or Big Talk or one of the band members' solo albums. Brandon Flowers, for instance, has released two chart-topping solo albums. This song is from…one of them?

The search engine knows it. Andreas has his tablet finish the verse.

The woman's dark eyes seem to disappear under the lids. "Uh-huh," she intones. "Cute." Her eyes dart back to York. "What about you? Are you a dreamer?"

York's eyes widen. "Oh! Oh! I know who you are!"

"Do you now?" the woman croons.

"You're ICE!" he exclaims. "No, I'm a natural-born US citizen. Besides, Dreamers are legally protected." York smiles at Andreas as he affectionately parrots his brother's repeated refrain: "That's the law!"

The woman stares at the duo, slack-jawed. "N-No! I am *not* ICE!" But, suddenly, her jaw snaps shut, and she slips back into her act. It's such a bad act that even Andreas knows it's an act, and he's been repeatedly told that he's a terrible actor. "But I can be, if you'd like me to—"

York pulls away as she moves to touch him again. "Why would I want you to be ICE?" His voice cracks. "ICE is *terrible!*" His eyes dart wildly. "I-I mean, I love the United States government!"

"Sweetheart, you're on The Strip," the woman deadpans.

"I am aware of that!" York yelps. "And I am starting to think that I should not be!"

Andreas starts and shows his brother the collection of links to activities they had assembled. *"But look at all the things we planned to do!"*

"But do you want to do *any* of it? We have a limited amount of time. We need to spend it on—"

The woman clears her throat.

York swerves on her. "None of the things involve anyone else but us!"

Harrumphing, she stomps off. York shrinks in on himself. "Ah, no, I shouldn't have yelled!" Before he can gather the courage to apologize, though, she has disappeared.

In the meantime, Andreas has thought about his brother's question. He wants to see tigers, but not really because he's seen in movies and in the news that tigers can hurt people. Baby tigers can't, but Las Vegas isn't the only place with baby tigers. Besides, Las Vegas hurts baby tigers. Baby tigers don't belong in suitcases! Baby tigers belong… Well, Andreas can't go to the wild, but he *can* go to a zoo. If he wants to. Tigers in zoos don't hurt people, right?

"No," Andreas tells York, informing him of his agreement: He too is starting to think that he should not be here, and there is no one else they need to consult if they want to leave but themselves.

York's face lights up. "Good! Then we're decided! And no one is waiting for us! So, we can leave!"

Andreas's brow furrows. *"What would we do if someone was waiting for us?"*

"Well, we'd need to stay and wait for them," York states empathetically. "We can't be rude!"

"Rude?" Andreas questions. *"Like…"*

York cuts him off. "She interrupted our conversation first! She was the rude one!"

* * *

"We need to go places we actually *want* to go to," York announces once they are in the car, escaping from The Strip. "We have a limited amount of time. We need to use it doing things that actually *matter* to us."

Ah, the time limit is a classic plot: the aliens need to be defeated on Independence Day. And if York doesn't return Andreas to Ridgecrest in time for school, their mother will be right: York doesn't deserve to get into college, and Andreas can't do anything.

If their mother is right, he will never have independence again.

"Which is why," his older brother continues, "we need to go see The Killers."

Andreas glares at him. *"Didn't you say we need to go to places* we *actually want to go to? I don't want to see The Killers!"* He ratchets up the volume to give emphasis to his words, even though it hurts York's ears. Then, something occurs to him. *"Aren't they on tour anyway?"* He is not actually sure if the band is on tour, but from what he knows about bands, that is what they do most of the time.

"Oh, I see the confusion!" York exclaims. "I don't want to see them in concert, Skippy. I want to see the things The Killers have talked about. Look up…" His front teeth—and the gap between them—glint in a determined grin. "…The Victims' Pilgrimage."

Andreas thinks that sounds like a step-to-step guide to death, but to his relief, he finds an old Blogspot account with half of the images broken. Even if his brother wants to take this pilgrimage to victimhood, he cannot follow the instructions!

"The website is broken," Andreas informs him. And what a shame!

"But the place they're from isn't!" York fishes out his Nevada packet. Andreas swats at him because those are *his* maps, and the rule is that people can only touch their *own* things! York at least has the respect to look apologetic. "Sorry. I just need… Look for Henderson. Henderson, Nevada. That's where they're from."

Andreas takes a long time examining the map, but sure enough, no matter how hard he squints, Henderson is intact on the map. Darn.

"Come on, Skippy, we saw how *not* fabulous Las Vegas is. Don't you want to see how many more things The Killers are wrong about so you can prove me wrong?"

It *is* a tempting offer, but what Andreas really wants is to tell The Killers what they said wrong, so they can stop misleading their victims! The boy hums noncommittally.

York seizes the opportunity to sweeten the deal: "We can take turns picking places! You'll be next!"

Andreas has no idea where he wants to go next, but he trusts his ideas more than York's! And while York is dithering about his Victims' tour, Andreas can give some important time to his ideas. Which would be better than this. Even if he didn't have any time to think about it. *"Deal!"* he decides. The boy extends his arm to "shake on it."

"Skippy, I'm driving."

And neither of them wants to go to a hospital, so Andreas shakes his own hand to confirm the transaction.

* * *

To York's shock, there is not a Killers museum in Henderson, Nevada—nor in any of the towns between Las Vegas and Henderson, according to the hour's worth of road signs, which should have only been a half-hour's worth, according to Andreas's maps. "But!" he blubbers. "This is where Brandon Flowers grew up!" When Andreas looks it up on the Internet, the first result he gets is for a "Museum of Death" in New Orleans, Louisiana.

The same state that doesn't believe in counties. An untrustworthy state.

The Museum of Death's website is old but not broken. He does not mention it to his brother, lest he decide that it should be a location on their list. Andreas doesn't trust any museum that boasts "falling down ovations" as a selling point.

"Falling down ovations" means fainting.

"Now where is…Horizon Street…" York hums to himself as he twirls underneath the S Green Valley Parkway to a lyric video on Andreas's tablet.

Wait. Oh, no. Did the song just mention Las Vegas again? Why are musicians obsessed with the place? Andreas turns off the video and switches back to his text-to-speech software. *"We are not going back to Las Vegas!"*

"We're not!" York confirms. "Because look! There it is!"

Andreas squints against the sun. *"That says Glowing Horizon Street."*

"Creative liberties," York dismisses. He scampers past a housing development called The Canyons. "A young Brandon Flowers grew up here!"

"Somewhere *around here*," Andreas types sulkily.

His older brother nods thoughtfully. "When they make the museum about The Killers, I'm sure it will clarify our questions." Squealing in excitement, he spins and sings again—this time, a song called "Sam's Town," by The Killers. Although they're in Brandon's town.

The desert wind blows in their faces, and, with it, comes a mirage: a young woman, around York's age, wearing all black, with red eyeliner and bleached purple hair. "Hello!" she shouts. "I love that song!"

"Hi! I love it too!" York blinks rapidly. "Um…Maybe we should close the distance between us? I don't like shouting!"

"Good id—" She stops as she spots York and Andreas covering their ears. She traipses up to the duo and beams, bouncing on her heels. "Wild to meet another fan out here! My name's Charlotte!"

Andreas's attention is immediately drawn to her hands. She's clicking something. Suddenly, a pair of dark eyes are staring back at his. "Oh, if I'd known you wanted a cube too,

I would have brought more than one in my purse! As it is, my spare is in my hotel room."

"We-We'd never take something that isn't ours!" York stammers, instinctively breaking her eye contact with Andreas by waving his hand in front of the young woman's face. Except...He would. Because he did. York took his maps. "We follow the law!"

"Oh, I do too!" Charlotte chirps. "Which is why I won't invite you back to my hotel room to get it! You aren't allowed to do that to minors! How old are you, fourteen?"

"Twelve," Andreas answers, impressed by her guess.

"I knew it!" she squeals. "Minor! I knew by the lack of facial hair!" She stops. "Wait, but I'm eighteen, and I don't have facial hair..."

Andreas rubs his bare chin self-consciously. He knows his father is hairy, and York has to shave regularly, so he'll have a beard like Gandalf one day...

"Don't worry, Skippy," York says. "It'll come in eventually."

"Skippy?" Charlotte asks, pulling herself out of a thinking spiral by her bootstraps. "Is that your name? I love your robot voice, by the way!"

Andreas shakes his head. *"My name is Andreas. This is my brother, York. I've never had anyone say 'robot voice' nicely before."*

She grins, and Andreas sees the shine of a retainer on both sets of teeth. "Then everyone is silly! Robots are awesome! Don't you think, Andreas and York?"

The brothers nod in agreement. "Do you two also think The Killers are awesome?" While Andreas shakes his head, York nods. Charlotte giggles. "One out of two isn't bad! That's half-full!" Andreas's mathematical argument about one out of two being as bad as it is good fizzles on his tongue as he catches sight of it again: the clicking cube in her hands! What is it? "Hey, if you guys—er, guy—like The Killers, did you come looking for where they're from? I'm from the next town over, so I've done some digging around myself—"

"Hey, you!" a shrill voice calls from an open window of The Canyons luxury apartments. "This here is private property! I'm giving you lying punk trolls sixty seconds to scram before I call the police!"

The brothers look between each other in fright. Charlotte, by contrast, clicks her cube faster. "Uh oh. Well, good thing I was just about to ask this: Do you two want to go to The Cheesecake Factory for dinner? Around six?"

York and Andreas look at each other incredulously. How can she think about cheesecake at a time like this? Or think about cheesecake at any time? They don't like cheesecake!

"I'll bring my other cube!" Charlotte adds.

Oh, that? That is convincing. Maybe, then, at dinner, she can say what these clicking cubes are? Also, dinner. Dinner is good. Before the duo can question Charlotte any further, though, she's running away, bellowing, "Scatter!"

CHAPTER 7

————

"So, your music tour was a bust," Andreas says. *"That doesn't mean that our next destination has to be. Especially since I'm picking it!"*

"I wouldn't call it a failure," York chides. "I found the street he grew up on! Supposedly! And…I must admit to being interested in going to a cheesecake factory."

Andreas frowns. *"But we don't like cheesecake,"* he punches out on the keypad authoritatively. He is curious about Charlotte's clicking cubes, but he doesn't like cheesecake, and she talked about The Killers the whole time, and Andreas doesn't like The Killers.

"I know!" York exclaims. "But aren't you interested to see how it all goes wrong?"

Well, seeing how things go wrong is always interesting. Besides, Charlotte *is* expecting them. Andreas knows he won't convince York to leave a social obligation behind—he already pushed his luck convincing him to leave their mother and *stay* leaving. And, to his surprise, Andreas doesn't want to leave this social obligation behind either. Charlotte *liked* his robot voice! The best response he had ever had to his tablet before was ignoring it, and the person who ignored it is gone now.

For a moment, Andreas gets lost in the memory of her—Raleigh. She listened to him when they talked, not the stilted stutters of the tablet, and then, all of a sudden, she was gone. But the important part is that Raleigh was his friend, and maybe Charlotte could be York's friend. They both like the same bad music. That's how friends start, right? Liking the same thing?

He can't ignore that.

Andreas puts in the address for the Cheesecake Factory. The setting sun casts the manicured lawns they drive past in an unnatural pallor. Andreas supposes that makes sense: The lawns *are* unnatural. Lawns don't live in the desert! They pull into the driveway at 6 p.m. exactly. At 6:05 p.m., York decides to turn off the car to save gas. At 6:06 p.m., the music cuts out, leaving them to wait in silence, futzing with their respective electronic devices. They spot the familiar shock of purple hair at 6:30.

"Sorry about that," Charlotte exclaims. "But I set my alarm for leaving at 6 for 6! I know, it's terrible, but I can make it up to you." She drops two gray cubes with red buttons into the car.

Andreas scoops one up. It's one of her clicking cubes! But wait—didn't she say she only had one spare?

Charlotte flashes her own clicking cube. "I thought I had lost my back-up spare, but nope! Good luck, isn't it?"

York shakes his head vehemently. "You can't just give us your things! I mean, I've never seen anything like this! It must be rare!"

Charlotte's brow furrows. "Just because you've never seen anything like this before doesn't mean it's rare. I lose my fidget cube all the time, so I've bookmarked Antsy Labs' website!"

Andreas searches for the name *Antsy Labs* and finds an image of the object in his hand—a "fidget cube"—and then the same object in different colors: blue, yellow, pink, green, and more. And then cubes shaped like superheroes!

York gasps. "Oh, my goodness, is that Baby Groot?"

Charlotte nods. "I don't how they landed a deal with Marvel, but I told myself that if I don't lose my current one this year, I'll get an Iron Man fidget cube next year! I know they're the same price, but I'd feel sadder that I lost Iron Man than if I lost…gray. I don't get attached to colors."

The young woman peers at the restaurant. "Oh, good, we're before the dinner rush. Or the dinner rush isn't coming today." She shrugs. "People are weird. There's no way to predict them!"

York looks embarrassed, but Andreas, emboldened by the superhero relic in his hands, speaks up. *"We don't like cheesecake."*

Charlotte smiles. "I don't like cheesecake either! But this place has over 250 things on its menu! You're bound to like *one* of them!"

* * *

Charlotte confidently orders a plain cheese pizza. York tentatively orders the same thing.

Andreas, on the other hand, is intrigued by the "Super Foods" section of the menu. Will it give him superpowers? Reading the description of the "Wellness Salad," he thinks not, but he knows that a plain cheese pizza will have no vegetables, so it will be good to have some to spare.

As their food arrives and Andreas furtively puts some leafy greens to the side of his brother's pizza, though, he finds that the only superpower he wants right now is Charlotte's confidence. All his life, Andreas has been told that not looking someone in the eye shows that you are both rude and meek. Charlotte's eyes wander between her fidget cube and the menu and the ceiling fan, but she smiles through it all, shoulders loose. And through it all, she hasn't stopped clicking her fidget cube. Their waitress gave her a long look, but Charlotte ordered a refill of her water without breaking her rhythm.

Andreas always feels wrong clicking his fingernails together and drumming them against his desk, and the fidget cube is less quiet than his hands! York's spinning is quieter than both Andreas's hands and Charlotte's fidget cube, but Andreas knows that York has gotten yelled at for spinning more than he has for clicking.

Their mother says York can "just be normal." She never says that about Andreas.

Andreas wonders what their mother would say about Charlotte, with her fidget cube. She doesn't have calm hands.

As it would turn out, York is wondering the same thing because he asks, "Do your parents know that you have a fidget cube?"

"Well, my parent bought me my first one. I've been paying for the other ones, though!" Charlotte laughs. "Being eighteen sucks. Before, I could tell them that I legally *couldn't* buy anything online."

York nods in agreement. "Nothing *happens* on your eighteenth birthday," he says. "Except what everyone else has decided must happen."

"You get it!" Charlotte gasps. "Like nothing happens on your thirteenth birthday!"

"*Something happens on your thirteenth birthday,*" Andreas pipes up. "*You become a teenager.*"

Andreas doesn't like the laugh they share. He seizes the opportunity to change the subject. "*What brings you to Henderson?*"

Charlotte's eyes light up. "Oh, I'm glad you asked! I'm starting to go to Nevada State College in the fall, so my parent thought it would be wise for me to spend some time in its city by myself, even though we don't live far. I'm going to be studying engineering!"

York looks away. "Oh...You...You know what you want to study? Already?"

"Well, yeah! I've always loved science and computers, and my parent is a huge fan of Nevada State College! They have Nevada's first Bachelor of Arts in Deaf Studies! Since they're an ASL interpreter, they follow news like that!"

Andreas looks at the fidget cube in his hands. It takes up a lot of space in his hands, and he's not even fidgeting with it, so how do Charlotte's hands have room to sign? He sets his fidget cube in the space between him and his brother. "*Do you know American Sign Language?*" he asks.

"Well, I understand it way better than I speak it, since my hands like to do different things, but..." Charlotte passes the fidget cube to her other hand. She raises her hand to her forehead, her thumb touching it, then puts her thumb out.

York looks at the sign intensely.

Charlotte beams. "That's 'hello' in ASL!" she explains.

York copies the sign. Andreas gauges Charlotte's reaction to York's sign before attempting it himself. "Yeah!" she cries. "I don't practice as much as I should, but when I'm unable to talk, ASL comes in handy."

Andreas looks at his tablet. If it were to run out of battery or get broken, then he wouldn't be able to talk...

But Charlotte has moved on. "But wait a second. I need to ask the same question: What brings you two to Henderson?"

"We're going on a road trip!" Andreas answers, turning the volume on his tablet louder to emulate an excited shout. *"We're making our way east! Like pioneers!"* Wait, no. The pioneers went from east to west, not west to east. *"Or...The opposite of them!"*

Charlotte shakes her head. "But you *are* pioneers! You're going all the way to the East Coast? Where exactly? And why?"

"I'm going to college there. On the East Coast, I mean," York admits shyly. "The College of Saint Rose, in Albany, New York."

Andreas looks up the school's website and hands his tablet to Charlotte, who gapes in wonder. "Whoa! So cool! And I'm not even leaving Nevada to go to college!" She gasps. "Wait, you'll be a freshman too?"

"Me too!" Andreas huffs. *"In high school! After this year!"*

Charlotte grins. "Then we *have* to exchange contact information. We can talk about school and fidget cubes!"

Andreas knows he won't be allowed to bring his fidget cube to school, but he's intrigued to see how Charlotte will do.

* * *

Charlotte insists on paying for the brothers' meal at The Cheesecake Factory—"since I made you try it." She then takes the brothers to her hotel. While she explains that she can't let them into her room—One of you is a minor, and both of you are boys. My parent says I can't have boys in my room until I'm out of college. I don't get it, since that isn't a law, but the minor one is!"

It is perfectly within the law, though, for York to buy a hotel room for him and Andreas, however.

* * *

York is worried about the handle on the shower, so he lets Andreas try it first. It's very nice of York, to let Andreas be able to get into his pajamas first. The rule is that you cannot get into your pajamas until after your shower. That rule was made because people love pajamas, and showering is important, so if you can only wear your pajamas after your shower, you will do it, even if you don't love showering.

Or you can't figure out how to make your shower warm.

Andreas yelps as the water comes out cold. He starts wildly hitting the handle, and, one time, he realizes that he can lift the handle, not just push it down, and the water shifts from freezing to balmy. Andreas hums in satisfaction.

He spaces out for a while, but there is more to taking a shower than warm water! There is soap! Soap in his hair! He squeezes his eyes shut as he runs his fingers through his short, blond hair. Even though his eyes are closed, he knows that there is soap in his hair because he can hear the hiss of the bubbles. It is good that his hair is short. Because he has less hair, he needs less soap.

How much soap does Gandalf need for his facial hair?

How much soap does *York* need for his head hair?

He needs both soap *and* water, so Andreas needs to save some for him!

Andreas steps out of the stall, reaches in, and pushes the handle down, back to a neutral position. The water stops flowing. The soapy residue swirls down the drain.

After Andreas finishes drying up, he hops up to his brother, jumping over the splintered tile of the bathroom and skirting around the mysterious stains on the carpet of the bedroom. York is squatting on the bed closer to the bathroom, staring intently at a blank text message.

"I figured out the warm water," Andreas is happy to report. *"Do you want me to show you?"* Andreas sneaks a peek at his brother's phone. Charlotte has sent York a picture of Tony Stark—also known as Iron Man—and the kid who is also Spider-Man talking.

It seems like York is still trying to figure out how to respond to the picture. While Charlotte appears to be a Marvel fan, York has never seen a Marvel movie before.

York sighs. "Yes, please."

His phone screen suddenly goes blank, except for the phone icon and the name of the person calling: *Mom.* The brothers look at each other. They both know that their mother will not accept them being in the shower—or the phone being on silent—for a reason why they did not answer her call.

The shower can wait. This is more important. Andreas climbs into his brother's bed as York swipes to accept the call and pushes the button for the speakerphone.

"What have you even eaten today?" she demands. "You'll need to come home if you want to eat some real food!"

Andreas winces. Their mother has a good point. Ice cream—no matter from what gas station—is not an appropriate breakfast. But now that they know that they like tapsilog, that's something they can order from restaurants!

"We just ate dinner," York tells her. "Have you ever been to The Cheesecake Factory?"

"Cheesecake is not a dinner!"

Andreas made that same mistake, so he must correct it. *"The Cheesecake Factory is a restaurant. It has over 250 things on its menu."* And, out of over-250 things, why would she think that they would order something that they know they do not like?

"Andreas had a salad!" York adds helpfully because his own dinner—pizza—is not helpful.

"And how did you *pay* to eat at this restaurant?"

Andreas furrows his brow. With money? How else? Granted, they didn't use their own money this time, but does their mother really think they left to go across the country without any money? Or, worse, that they resorted to breaking the law to get money?

"Charlotte paid."

Andreas stares at his brother incredulously. Why would he say that?

Their mother reacts just as he knew she would: "You *mooched* off of someone?" To their mother, mooching is the peak of rudeness.

"It's not mooching if she offered to pay!"

"*She?*"

Andreas suddenly feels like they are being very rude to have screeching on speakerphone in a hotel. He taps the button to turn off speakerphone and holds York's phone up between their ears. Their mother is loud enough for them to hear.

"Who is she?"

"Like I said, her name is Charlotte. We met when I was singing a song, and she knew the next verse! Then, we got to talking, and she invited me and Andreas to dinner—"

"Oh. So, she was desperate."

Andreas watches as the color leaves his brother's face. "What did you say?"

"She was desperate. She asked the first guys she saw out, even though you have no idea what you're doing, and Andreas is twelve."

"No!" York snaps. "It's not a desperate thing to want to make friends! It's not a desperate thing to want to make friends with *us!* She sang a song with me! She complimented Andreas on his voice! She showed us her fidget cube! She *gave* us fidget cubes! You say she's desperate. Why are you so desperate to think that everyone wants to be mean?" He hangs up.

Andreas leaps to his feet. Yes! Yes, this is what he wanted from York on the last call: to put his foot down, as an adult, and say that their mother is wrong! If their mother thinks that she's wrong, then maybe she'll be quiet and let Andreas wait six years in peace for nothing to happen on his eighteenth birthday, nothing but the numb relief of escape suddenly being sanctioned.

Then, Andreas gets the last thing he wants: tears. His brother is crying. "Is she right, Skippy? Is Charlotte *desperate?*"

The phone has flicked back to the screen it was on before: the text from Charlotte. *"Why don't you ask her?"*

"What? Ask if she's desperate?"

"No," Andreas answers. *"Ask if she's our friend."*

York does. Charlotte texts back "yes" and a GIF of Tony Stark smiling. *"Proof,"* Andreas declares triumphantly.

York sniffles. "Dad's right. Mom has a real way of getting under your skin."

Andreas blinks rapidly. Their father? York is acting like he has talked to him, but they only "talk" on their birthdays and the Christmas season, and, even then, primarily through letters.

"He said he'll show us around New York City, you know," York quips.

Andreas doesn't remember that. He read the letter from his last birthday and he knows that, for a few years now, he and York have been getting the same letter. Unless York isn't talking about a letter. *"We are going to Albany,"* he broaches.

York falls for it. "New York City's on the way. Dad said we could stay in his apartment for a bit. It's in Bronx."

"The *Bronx*," Andreas corrects numbly. When did he and York talk? *Why* did he and York talk? His brother made a deal with him that they would make their agenda for this trip together! They shook on it! That's the law for deals!

"Mom has told us for years that Dad is bad, but he *has* to be better than her."

No. There is neither a rule nor a law about that. Getting hit with fire is bad, but even if you don't get hit by fire, you can still get hit by lava. Andreas re-examines his brother. The call with their mother has drained him. It's like he's melting. York can't get hit by the truth right now. He won't understand. Just like he doesn't understand about the man who kicked Stormy.

York doesn't understand. He wasn't trying to hurt Andreas by saying that he doesn't understand. He was trying to help in the way he knows how. That's okay. Andreas doesn't always know how to help, like that time two or three years ago, when his brother came home from that party and blubbered something about how he had a bad time? Come the next morning, York said he never wanted to talk about it again. If you don't like something, you don't want to talk about it. If you're still worried about something, you *never* want to talk about it. But because Andreas didn't know what it was that was worrying his brother, he didn't know how to help. So, he never talked about it.

With that revelation, the anger pools at his feet like wax, spent.

"*You can put on your pajamas,*" Andreas offers.

York allows himself to fall back into his pillows. "I'll take a shower in the morning. Can you show me how the warm water works, though? Real quick?"

CHAPTER 8

———

Andreas drinks up the image of dried grass, the truth of Nevada's landscape, under the discerning eye of the mid-morning sun. Having slept on the question of where to go next, when York and Andreas get into the car, Andreas asks, *"Have you ever heard of Granpa Rex Allen?"*

York blinks rapidly. "We don't have a grandpa named Rex Allen."

"We don't," Andreas confirms. *"And we don't have a cat named Granpa Rex Allen either."*

"Skippy, I've already told you: We can't keep a cat in the car—"

"I don't want to keep a cat in the car!" the boy exclaims. *"I want to learn from Grandpa Rex Allen about how to keep cats alive!"* He rubs at the crack on his tablet's screen with his left hand while he touches the scar on his right cheek with his other hand.

The color drains from his older brother's face. "Where does Granpa Rex Allen live?" he asks reverently.

"Granpa Rex Allen is dead. He was thirty-four years old." At the look of befuddlement on his brother's face, Andreas

sighs. *"That's very old for a cat,"* he explains.

"Granpa Rex Allen is a cat? Did he come with that name?"

Andreas shrugs. *"If he did, that must have helped keep him alive,"* he posits. If he had named Atlas *Granpa Atlas,* he would have had to live up to the name, right? Like how babies named *Nana* grow up to be grandmothers. Not all of the oldest cats he looked up had names fit for old cats, but such a title couldn't hurt! *"While Granpa Rex Allen is now dead, we know where he was born: Paris, Texas."*

"Texas? That's quite a ways away." The space between York's eyebrows pinches as he looks out at the sandy streets ahead of them, as if he is trying to spot Texas on the horizon.

"We're still heading east!" Andreas presses. He shows his brother the map. *"Paris is in the northeast edge of Texas! Unlike Austin, which is more south. Austin is where Granpa Rex Allen's owner still lives."* Among 790,389 other people, according to the U.S. Census. *"But we don't need to go to Austin!"* Andreas hastily explains. *"I have pored through the interviews with Jake Perry. He cites bacon, eggs, broccoli, coffee, and nature documentaries as the key to Granpa Rex Allen's and Creme Puff's long lives."*

"Ooh, good to know..." York murmurs. "Do you think you still get the long life without the broccoli, though?" He frowns. "I don't like broccoli."

Andreas narrows his eyes. *"Creme Puff ate broccoli, even though her name was literally Creme Puff. If she could manage it, I'm sure you can."*

York makes a noncommittal hum. "What's good for a cat can be good for a human, right?"

Andreas answers his brother's question with another question: *"Is cat food good for humans?"*

"Well, no." York is quick to justify himself, however. "But

cats in the wild don't eat cat food! They eat meat and fish! Humans eat meat and fish!" Andreas knows that not all humans eat meat and fish, but he likes meat and fish. York has a good point. "Anyway, how old is Creme Puff?"

"Creme Puff was thirty-eight years and three days old when she died, so she holds the record for the oldest cat in the world. When she died, she was 168 years old in human time."

"Wait." York types something on his phone. "Isn't the oldest person only 120 years old?"

As if *only 120 years old* is something unimpressive. Jeanne Calment was 122 years and 164 days old.

Still a whippersnapper compared to Creme Puff, though. Andreas nods. *"Unfortunately, we don't know where Creme Puff was born, so Granpa Rex Allen's birthplace is the next best thing."*

York nods. "We'll have to get bacon and eggs there!"

Huh. That's an excellent idea actually.

"Let me just text Charlotte that we're heading out," York murmurs. Andreas peers over his shoulder to see Charlotte send a GIF of someone waving and an invitation to hang out and maybe meet her parent on their way back westward.

* * *

Having encountered some unexpected traffic—Although they didn't have an expectation about where they would go next, they at least expected that they would get there on time!—York and Andreas find themselves driving into Paris, Texas later than they'd hoped.

This late at night, it is to be expected that most restaurants are closed. But they locate Mckee's 24-Hour Family Restaurant—and it is exactly what it says on the sign. It's open twenty-four hours a day, they're serving a family, and it's a restaurant.

Their waiter is even named Mickey! (It is a different spelling, but the brothers test the pronunciation, and even Andreas's tablet agrees that they are the same sound.)

"Well, if you're done experimenting with my name, what can I get for you?" Everything Mickey has said has been in the form of a long, sighing exhale.

"Bacon and eggs!" York exclaims, eager to taste supercentenarianism.

"Is that the 'One Egg & Bacon' on the menu or the 'Two Eggs & Bacon'?"

Andreas peers at the fine print. *"Two Eggs & Bacon,"* he answers for his brother. While he dug into their cereal supply for lunch while in the traffic jam, he knows that York has not eaten anything since breakfast. *"This says this is served with hash browns, toast, and jelly. Can we have our food with broccoli, coffee, and nature documentaries?"*

"No broccoli on mine!" York cuts in.

Mickey blinks slowly. "Go wild with the TV," he says, tossing them a grimy TV remote. "We don't serve broccoli here, but I can get your coffee. It comes with free refills."

As York flips through the channels, Andreas watches as a cloud tucks the moon in for bed. *"Can you put the coffee in a to-go cup?"* he asks. He nods at York. *"It can be part of our breakfast tomorrow."*

"Coffee *is* a breakfast!" York insists.

Andreas looks to Mickey for support. "Don't look at me. You're the guys eating bacon and eggs for dinner. It is literally my job not to judge you, though."

He has a good point. The boy hums in consideration. *"Do you think the long life works if you eat in reverse?"* At twin confused expressions, he explains. *"Granpa Rex Allen lived to thirty-four because he ate bacon and eggs for breakfast. Do you think it works if we eat bacon and eggs for dinner?"*

"Thirty-four, huh? Dream big, kids."

"Thirty-four is very old for a cat," Andreas informs him.

"Whatever." Mickey stalks off.

Free of their waiter's judgment, Andreas repeats the question to York. "I don't know," the teen answers. "We have the nature documentary, though. That should work at all hours."

The brothers push their bacon and eggs to opposite sides of the plate as the big cat cubs push their mothers to opposite sides of the kill.

As a commercial plays, York checks the time on his phone. "Oh, wow, we need to sleep." When he shows his brother the time, Andreas agrees. "Before we pay and pull into a motel, though, I was wondering if you have any plans for tomorrow."

"Drink coffee for the first time," Andreas jokes.

"You're a liar, Skippy," York laughs. "I know you've taken some of Mom's coffee before. But tell me the truth: Do you have any other cat-related places in mind?"

"I don't have any other places in mind," the twelve-year-old confesses.

York grins. "Then maybe you'd be open to my idea."

"As long as it isn't about The Killers..."

"It's not!" York assures him. "It's about cats." York puts his hands on the table and accentuates his dramatic pauses with pointing, first to himself, next to Andreas, then occupying his hands with imitating cat claws. "Let me ask you: What do cats love?"

"Hunting." The brothers look. This lion pride has learned to hunt giraffes.

"True," York admits in a gasp of awe. He tears his gaze away from the TV. "But what else do cats love?"

"*Sleeping.*" The male lion yawns, although he didn't do any giraffe-hunting.

"Maybe I'm mistaken, then," York wonders out loud. He drops his hands underneath the table. "Do cats like yarn?"

"*Atlas didn't, but I do!*" Andreas cries excitedly.

Beaming, York shows him a picture of The World's Largest Ball of Twine. "We'll be a bit too early for the Twine-a-Thon—"

"*What's a Twine-a-Thon?*"

"I don't know, but I'm sad that we'll be missing it. What do you think, though?"

"*There's no point in seeing the birthplaces of cats that lived less long...*" Andreas demurs. "*I want to see the longest! The biggest! The highest! The -est-est!*"

* * *

The search for the biggest ball of twine in the United States brings York and Andreas to Cawker City, Kansas. As they drive through the town, they notice that the sidewalks have a thread of twine painted on them, bleached by the sunlight. They may be out of the desert, but the plains still have precious few trees to shield from the sun's rays, and the buildings, unlike in, say, Las Vegas, are short and cast shadows that one needs to squeeze into. Still, Andreas is focused on the painted twine. Maybe they lead to the twine ball—which is hopefully not painted itself.

Since the twine road isn't on the car road, though, they need to get out to follow the sidewalks! They pull into an empty lot next to a church. It isn't Sunday, so no one will be in there.

"There!" Andreas points down at the faded asphalt. *"Follow me!"*

The twine stripe weaves its way through Wisconsin Street. Andreas splays his arms out and hops along the painted-on, windy path.

"Told you so," the boy hears as a gust of wind tries to blow him off his tightrope.

York drifts off the path to examine a collection of paintings in the front window of one of the stores. "Hey, Skippy? Does this painting look…off to you?"

Andreas leaps off the twine-tightrope then scampers over to his brother. *"Why is the man in the painting screaming about a yarn ball?"*

York studies the painting. A man is on a wooden boat, his hands up to his face. "I don't know," he must confess. "But he's not facing the thing he's screaming."

Andreas hums. *"Maybe it's too scary?"* He enters into the search engine on his tablet "painting man screaming" and discovers a painting called *The Scream*, but it can't be the same painting because there is no yarn ball in it!

As they push farther down the street, though, they discover why the man in the painting is screaming about a yarn ball. The world's largest ball of twine is huge: a lumpy mass that contains over 1,500 miles of twine. Andreas steals a glance at his United States map. If he tried to unravel the ball, he would still be unraveling twine as he traipsed into the Pacific Ocean.

Which would certainly make it smell worse. And it already smells *terrible*. The brothers recoil as a gust of wind sends the scent toward them in a full assault.

As they raise their shirts over their noses, though, they suddenly press their hands against their mouths, stifling gasps.

A young girl, who looks to be no more than seven, takes a spool of twine and wraps it around the ball. The other girl with her, who looks just like her, except for the fact that she is wearing a purple dress instead of a pink one, is urging her to run faster, but she doesn't see the knot of abandoned twine on the ground, so she trips into the arms of a matronly woman, who chuckles at her. The pink-dress girl, her cheeks red with embarrassment at her clumsiness, returns the spool to her.

Someone...just *added* to the world's largest ball of twine!

The matronly woman who handed the girls the spool turns around. Her sun-worn face splits into a grin. "Hello! Did you two call or email ahead?" Andreas and York shake their heads. "Oh, don't worry about it!" she exclaims. "I already have my spooler out, so you can step right up!"

The brothers step back. "But it isn't the Twine-a-Thon?" York offers.

She jerks her head back in laughter. "The Twine-a-Thon is just our town fair! You can add to the ball at any time! I like to get a notification at least a day in advance, but..." She shrugs. "I always keep my spools in my trunk!"

"How many people add to the ball?" Andreas offers tentatively.

"Come and see for yourself! We keep record books!" She flourishes at a frayed guest book.

Pinching his nose with one hand, Andreas leafs through the guest book with the other. As he feels York come up behind him, Andreas looks at him sadly.

"But..." York murmurs. "This isn't fair. Of course, you're the biggest. You keep adding to it."

The woman huffs. "Our twine ball has evolved to be more than the work of just one man! It's a community effort!"

York pulls back. "It's a great community effort! It's just… not what we're looking for. You can't be the biggest twine ball if you're always getting bigger. It's unfair. Other twine balls are locked away, in museums, unable to ever get bigger." He looks down at his brother, who nods in confirmation.

"You can leave, then!" she harrumphs. "As long as you don't go to the Branson Ball! They *sold* it to Ripley!" She brims with pride. "We held on to our integrity."

Andreas blinks curiously as he finds an article from *The Atlantic*: "Twisted: The Battle to Be the World's Largest Ball of Twine." He starts scrolling. York gasps with interest, but he sees how a growing number of people are glaring at them.

"*The Atlantic* will help us out," York agrees. "But let's have it help us in the car…" York and Andreas don't want to test the "integrity" of the people of Cawker City's anger.

* * *

"Nine hours and thirty minutes," the tablet booms.

York releases a pinched sigh. Andreas shifts to his text-to-speech app. *"Hey, that's what the GPS said, not me!"*

"Didn't we read about a ball in Missouri, though? Wouldn't it be faster than going to—" York pauses to review the article. "—Darwin, Minnesota?"

Ah, but York's question proves that he didn't pay attention while he was reading. Andreas huffs at him. It is true that the Branson Ball, as it is called in the twine industry, in Branson, Missouri, is closer to Cawker City, Kansas than Darwin, Minnesota, but its very name is wrong. The article itself features a photo that reveals the truth: that the so-called "Branson Ball" is not even ball-shaped!

You need to be a ball to be the biggest ball of twine! (Research reveals that yarn does not withstand the test of time, but Andreas is confident that cats can play with the sisal twine: the official twine of the biggest twine balls. The Branson Ball fails there too!)

They spend the next nine hours and thirty minutes driving. Sure, they eat and sleep and, yes, clean the car a little—The car isn't a garbage can!—outside that time. But mostly, Andreas passes the time by observing the sprouting of new trees on his side of the highway. And Andreas doesn't just mean "new to life." Indeed, although the first tree Andreas spots is a mere sapling, it is not long before he sees adult trees, and it dawns on him how new these trees are to him. These are cedars and pines, shaped like arrows, pointing up to the sky, not the frog-foot Joshua trees of Ridgecrest.

When York and Andreas arrive in Darwin, it's only the afternoon of the next day, but Andreas feels like they've flown through an alien portal.

Asking around town reveals that the ball is in a museum. It strikes Andreas that having their twine ball be out in the open, spewing its stench, is as alien to the people of Darwin as sealing their twine ball away to be hidden behind smeared glass is to the people of Cawker City.

Museums have opening and closing hours, but York and Andreas have never been to a museum that closes at 1 p.m., so there is only one question left to ask. "Where is the museum?" York inquires.

One of the 350 people in Darwin—according to the U.S. Census—guffaws. "Why don't you follow those fine folks?" They point, and the brothers watch as a red pick-up truck with a flapping Confederate flag on one end and a taped-on piece of cardboard on the other end claiming *Twine Ball or Bust!* speeds by, screeching into one of the blue-marked parking spots closest to a small, chick-yellow building.

"Fine folks?" York echoes, unconvinced. "Minnesota was never part of the Confederate—"

Never mind that! They've been outdone! *"Why didn't we get a sign?"*

"That is a good question," York confesses. "The better question is this." He turns back to the Darwin resident. "How often do people come through with Confederate flags?"

They answer his question with a question of their own: "Where are you from?"

"California," York offers tentatively.

They snort. "I knew it had to be that or New England."

"How do you know that?"

The Darwin resident sighs. "If you're not from one of the coasts, you're used to people with Confederate flags enough that you learn not to ask about them—or ask them anything."

"York!" Andreas exclaims. *"They just went inside! That must be where the twine ball is!"*

* * *

The brothers enter a small house that has been re-purposed into a museum, which talks about Francis A. Johnson, the builder of the twine ball. It's all very informative...except for one crucial detail.

"Excuse me," York pipes up. "Where is the twine ball? Is it in here?"

The man behind the reception desk chuckles. "No, it couldn't fit in here! You know Francis started construction inside his barn, but he had to move it outside!"

"*So, it's outside?*" Andreas remarks. The man lurches back at the sound of the mechanical voice. Andreas, for his part, turns to his brother. "*Let's check outside, then!*"

Outside, there is a gazebo resting on a ring of concrete, surrounded by a bed of grass. A trio of burly men with torn shirts and familiar red, white, and blue flags around their waists stomps on that grass, muscling past a teenage attendant to…huff at plexiglass?

"Please!" the teenage attendant exclaims. "Twine ball dust is bad for your lungs!"

"It's my brothers' *right* to do what they *want* to their lungs!" the shortest one, who is still six feet tall, bellows. "It's what our soldiers *fought* for!" He narrows his eyes at the young employee's nametag. "…*Charles.*"

Charles's gaze drifts toward the Confederate flags. "Actually, my ancestors were—"

"Patronizing Yankee! We can handle ourselves, boy!"

"—frontiersmen?" Charles finishes confusedly. "New Mexico wasn't even a state during the Civil War!"

"Mexico?" the men roar.

"New Mexico is a state *now!*" the teen squeaks.

Andreas uses the moment of distraction to scamper up to the plexiglass windows of the gazebo. "*Look, York! It's in there!*"

The trio whips around and stares at the boy with saucer-wide eyes. "Mexicans and robots… What has the North come to? Let's head home!" They pile into their truck and zoom off with equally reckless speeding.

Charles sighs in relief. "I assume you also want a whiff?"

Andreas shakes his head vigorously. "We just came from Cawker City, actually," York admits. "We've had enough of old-twine-smell to last us a lifetime."

"Cawker City, huh?" Charles says. "Don't say that too loudly around these parts. I've been to the Big Four, and I can confirm that the best twine ball is right here."

"*The Big Four?*" Andreas presses.

"Cawker City, Darwin, Branson, and Lake Nebagamon."

Andreas punches the name into his tablet. He shows the results to York: Lake Nebagamon is in Wisconsin.

York wants to shake his head, but Charles is looking at them with such *zeal* in his expression…"We've never been to Darwin before. Can you recommend a place to eat?"

Charles begins rattling off restaurants, which seems to calm him down. York tells him he will check them out. As the brothers walk back to their car, though, York sighs. "Are you also tired of yarn—er, *twine*—balls?"

"*The Atlantic said Cawker City's is the biggest, and Wisconsin is in the other direction,*" Andreas demurs. Although the street they're on is called Wisconsin Street, that doesn't necessarily mean it will provide a straight shot to Wisconsin! *"I think we've exhausted our twine-related destinations."*

As Andreas makes the declaration, York's phone begins vibrating violently. Curiosity piqued, Andreas peers at his brother's phone.

When he sees the name of the caller flash on the screen, Andreas instantly loses his curiosity. "What does she want to call desperate now?" York moans.

"*Why don't we just ignore her?*" Andreas recommends. "*We talked to her—*" One day ago? Two? "*—recently enough.*"

"I can't ignore Mom! She'll think I lost my phone or wasn't looking at it or flushed it down the toilet."

"*The only one who has done that is Mom,*" Andreas reminds York.

"I know! Which is why I don't take my phone out in bathrooms! But you know what I mean: if I ignore this call, it will because of something I did wrong, some reason that…that… *proves* that we really couldn't do it."

"Even if you did lose your phone, we still have my iPad. Phones have nothing to do with the success of road trips! Road trips existed far before phones!" Andreas reassures him. Sensing that his brother is more concerned about the recent past than history, he considers bringing up the car accident they drove past on the way to Cawker City. They could say that they were driving when she called! Calling while driving breaks the law!

But York is already pressing his phone to his ear and burying his fingers in his long, brown hair nervously. "Hello?" When he is sure that his brother is quiet, York secretly sets the phone on the dashboard and puts it on speakerphone.

"Where are you?" their mother demands.

Short questions should beget short answers. "Darwin, Minnesota," York replies mechanically.

"Minnesota? Isn't it—" She can't say what *it* is. As if *college* is a dirty word. "—in New York? I knew it! I knew it! You went the wrong way!"

Andreas's brow furrows. They have enough maps in the house. Surely, she knows that. She tried to stuff his maps under York's bed, so she must have felt how heavy his collection is.

York shrugs at Andreas. "Mom, there is only one way to get to New York: east."

No, Andreas needs to say something. *"If we went west from Ridgecrest, we would be in the Pacific Ocean. If we went north from Ridgecrest, we would be in Canada. If we went south from Ridgecrest, we would be in Mexico. We do not have passports, and cars cannot swim, so—"*

"The adults are speaking. I can hardly believe it myself, but your brother is nineteen, so—"

Andreas knows that if she hears him screaming, she'll scream back about how he needs to have calm hands. Even though it is his mouth that screams. Andreas storms out of the car. And then he screams. With his mouth.

When he turns around to sneak back into the car to continue to listen to the conversation, York is standing outside the car. "I'm not an adult until it's convenient for her, huh?" He shakes his head sadly. "And she can't listen to you when you're correct."

Relief washes over him. His brother understands this. That's what matters. *"That's why she never listens to me."*

York laughs. "Yet she believes that all of Minnesota has such terrible reception that..." He shows Andreas his phone screen. He has texted his mother that the phone reception is so terrible in the entire state of Minnesota that she must wait to call again until they are farther east. Andreas sees that the text has been marked as read.

"Where do you want to go next?" York asks with an easy smile.

"East!" Andreas declares authoritatively. They've established that it is the only correct way to go, after all. *"We've seen the brightest in The West. We've seen the biggest in The Middle. There has to be the something-est in The East!"*

CHAPTER 9

As they drive over to the other side of the Mississippi River, Andreas reaches down beneath his seat and ruffles through his packets. They're officially in "The East." However, before they go into "The Northeast"—home of New York, the City and Albany alike—there's at least one state he wants to go to.

"North Carolina, huh?" his brother pipes up. Andreas nods. "I've heard there's a famous mountain there!"

Andreas cocks his head. North Carolina doesn't have any of the United States' tallest mountains! They're all in Alaska!

"Hey!" York barks. "Just because it isn't tall doesn't mean it isn't famous!"

Andreas wishes they could drive to Alaska. He's seen pictures of The Northern Lights… Also, he wants to see if cats really can survive in Arctic conditions. If a cat can live to be thirty-four, cats can deal with a little snow, right? Unfortunately, he might need to ride on some dogs to get out into The Wild—poor dogs, forced to be out in the cold—but he's sure that there are buses to The Wild. The Wild is what Alaska is famous for, after all!

It occurs to Andreas that his North Carolina packet is no longer in his hands. It is in York's. The boy yelps. York had the nerve to talk about distracted driving when he had Stormy calmly on his lap and now his brother is *reading* while driving? The young man looks up from his reading and quirks an eyebrow at him. Confusion.

Implying driving while reading a map *isn't* distracted driving? Reading a map is like reading a text—except maps have lots of text. He whips his head, watching for the yellow solid line, which they are surely listing toward…Andreas doesn't see it.

"Looking for something?" York asks.

It occurs to Andreas that he doesn't feel anything bumping beneath him. He peers out the window. Nothing is moving past them. That means the car isn't moving at all! The boy unbuckles his seatbelt, so his body can fully express how he wants to *melt*. Of *course*, his brother wouldn't read a map while driving!

"Well, join the club," York continues. "There are lots of mountains in North Carolina." He brings the map closer to his face.

"That won't help." Andreas speaks from experience. Bringing the map closer to your face only makes the text smush together more.

"Then help me!" his brother whines. When Andreas outstretches his hands, he returns the map packet. He's wrinkled it. The boy feels his face wrinkle.

"Sorry. I did it again. I just got excited, you know?"

Andreas has the maps. York has the GPS. That's the rule. He needs a moment to drum out the anger sparking in his fingers, drumming like the spiky-haired man in York's favorite bands, backing up the thrumming guitar riff of his heart.

Wait, no, the heart pounds like a drum. Pounding a guitar doesn't work.

There's a reason why Andreas doesn't like that music. It's too confusing. For being sad, they're so *loud*. When York is truly upset, he goes completely quiet. Maybe their noise helps bring him back into some sort of balance? When Andreas is sad, he gets loud, but he's told that's "disruptive." Andreas needs to find out how to make money from *his* disruption.

Maybe he could sell his map-reading skills. Not to York, of course. He identifies that the mountains of The East, The Appalachian Mountains, are in North Carolina, specifically the section called The Blue Ridge Mountains. Andreas asks York if that sounds familiar.

He gives a noncommittal hum. "Maybe? What I remember is that the mountain had a family name."

"*A family name?*"

"A name for someone in your family."

Andreas looks back down at his map, but before his eyes even focus, he is asking, *"Mother?"*

York blinks. "No." Their mother has not called them back yet, thank goodness. Even though they're not in Minnesota anymore. Andreas ponders, considering that she did not know that New York is to the east, whether she knows how big Minnesota is.

As he deliberates, he continues trying to help York remember. *"Father?"* Does York remember what he and their father talked about? So, he could tell him?

"I feel like that's closer?" York encourages.

Closer than *Father?* What does that even mean? *"Uncle?"* Andreas tosses out.

"Now you're farther!"

What can be closer to a father than an uncle? Surely not a son. Not in their experience.

York cuts off his train of thought. "Wait. *Grandfather.* Is there a Grandfather Mountain?"

Andreas disagrees that a Grandfather is closer than an uncle to a father, but he does guide his brother's gaze to the western edge of the state.

"Whoa!" York gasps. "Do you think a lot of grandfathers go there?"

Andreas imagines that the hiking-oriented grandfathers, as few as they are, have a sense of humor.

"Cool. Then let's make it one of our stops."

As he tells his brother the town—Linville—and the trees begin to move again, he looks back down at his map. It will be four hours away. That's fine. Florists close early, but they open early too. That will give them time to travel. Unless Andreas wants to get the flowers for Raleigh as he gets closer to his destination? Surely there are florists in Raleigh. Andreas ponders that as the sunlight peeks through the oak trees off the highway.

* * *

They may have thought about time, but they may have forgotten to consider money. "That will be $44," the man at the gate says. In vain, Andreas checks his math. Alas, $22 per person means that the price for the two of them will be $44.

At the same time, though, they have just been thinking about the mountain. The sign advertises so much more: the Mile High Swinging Bridge, wildlife habitats, birding (Does that not happen inside the wildlife habitats?), daily programs, walking, and hiking (that's the same thing but okay). *Wonders Never Cease*, it proclaims. To be fair, Andreas is impressed that one of the highest suspension bridges in the United States—Google confirms the park's claim—is wheelchair-accessible! Considering that most *buildings* built before 1990 were not remodeled to fit within ADA guidelines, he is pleasantly surprised that the state of North Carolina chose to invest in remodeling a mountain. A mountain that was surely made before 1990. Before the 1900s, even! Maybe the trees are that old too: towering spruces whose needles turn upward at the ends of the branches, like open palms begging for sunlight. Andreas starts to dig into his wallet, a pouch he wears over his shoulder, so if someone tries to take it and run, they'll be dragging him with them, but York tells him that he's going to cover the costs. Andreas needs some money on him at all times—in case of an emergency.

His brother is right: There could be a map that they need anywhere!

They drive into the Grandfather Mountain Park and follow the line of cars—and the shouted directions of the employees—to their designated parking lot. "There are more people here than I expected," York admits as they slip out of the car. "What should we do first?"

Andreas weaves his way to the front of a clamoring camping group, badgering an employee distributing maps, and takes one without any fuss.

"Were you supposed to pay for that?" York asks.

The boy looks back at the camping group, getting louder and louder about their insistence that they're "seasoned professionals" and can "read the air," thereby "stamping out the fire cycle before it can even begin." Andreas looks down at the brochure. There are clearly marked locations where campfires are allowed…and clearly marked locations where they are not allowed.

"I can *pay for it,*" Andreas tells him.

"We can also pay by not lighting the mountain on fire," York decides, leading him away as the employee warns that the police will be called on park-goers who refuse the respect the rules stated clearly on the signs entering the facility. That includes not having campfires. Because no one wants the park on fire. So, yeah, that's their cue to leave.

Just in case, they both have money on them.

York seems set on taking his time. "Did you know that this park is part of the United Nation's international network of Biosphere Reserves?"

Well, it's not a lie, but also…"*What does that even* mean?"

His brother shrugs. "It's international, though! So, it's like we're traveling the world when we're really just traveling the country!"

York has a point: Unless they uncover alien wormholes, they are going to be short on international experiences on this trip.

Because he doesn't want anything else taking up the brain-space he needs for Raleigh's flowers, Andreas looks up what "the United Nation's international network of Biosphere Reserves" is. It's basically a place where people test ways to keep nature alive. Like by not allowing campfires.

Andreas doesn't like campfires. They're smoky and hot, and, really, you can make s'mores fine in a microwave. Maybe he can become part of "the United Nation's international network of Biosphere Reserves"!

Regardless of whether he earns that position, Andreas has his goal. "*We have to go to the bridge.*" Since Alaska is on the other side of Canada and neither of them have the paperwork set up for international travel, he had given up hope on going to the highest *anything*, since everything high is in Alaska. But this is one of the highest suspension bridges in the country! So, it's still high! Even though it's not in Alaska!

"Are you sure, Skippy? This brochure says it is over an eighty-foot chasm."

Well, they opted out of going to the lowest chasm in the country, but who cares about the lowest thing anyway? Height is what people talk about!

York is hyping up the Woods Walk. "The Woods Walk is a short, easy walk through a hardwood forest. This trail is excellent for small children and older folks," he reads from the brochure. "We'll find the hiking grandfathers!"

Andreas isn't quite convinced, though. Especially since this is the same brochure that warns on the next page: *Grandfather Mountain can host the region's most severe weather, including electrical storms, winds over 100 mph, deep snow and sub-zero cold. Weather can change quickly. Approach this mountain with respect—hikers have died here from falls, lightning, heart attacks and exposure. The best rule is: When bad weather strikes, leave the backcountry by trail as quickly and safely as possible.*

He shows his brother this page. He watches as the color drains from York's face. "*We* respect the mountain, though, right?"

"I *respect that the Mile High Swinging Bridge has an elevator. For a quick get-away.*" The seed of Andreas's plan finds fertile soil in York's mind. It is certainly helped by using the fertilizer of safety.

York acquiesces—on the condition that they stop if they see any animals on the way there. "I want to take pictures!" he exclaims, brandishing his phone.

Andreas's tablet is too old to take pictures. Not that he cares! It's not like it would be cool to include his own photographs in his map packets! To show how much he doesn't care, he harrumphs.

York doesn't care about how much he doesn't care. "Okay! Lead the way, Skippy!"

That, Andreas is happy to do. He starts running off toward the trail.

"Skippy, look—"

Andreas narrowly avoids a root poking through the path. He flashes a thumbs-up to his brother, but York doesn't care about that. "No running. You don't want to be unable to get to the bridge, right?"

If the park gives him access to a wheelchair if he twists his ankle, he'll be fine. That is what Andreas thinks. What Andreas says, though, is, *"Right."* Satisfied with the echo, York sets the slow but steady pace.

* * *

With how thick the forest is—which makes sense, considering they are in a nature reserve—they do not see the bridge so much as they see a crowd amassing. A man waving a flag is barking for the Linville United Methodist Church group to follow him, so he can teach them about the bridge before they cross it.

Andreas looks at his brother excitedly, but as the guide begins talking, he concludes that the guide isn't talking about the interesting parts. Andreas helps his brother by filling in the missing pieces: *"This bridge has been up since 1952. It was actually built in Greensboro, to test if it would work, before being re-built here—"*

"Psst! Skippy!" Andreas looks up from where he is reading from his tablet. Since most of the group members had gray to bald heads, he had assumed that they couldn't hear them. Either he miscalculated his tablet's volume, or he underestimated the group's ability to hear. Either way, they are staring at him. It is not a curious or even an amused stare. It is a calculating stare: a single assessment by a collective. It is like they are looking at a dog, trying to determine if it's merely lost or a threatening stray.

York seeks to assuage their concerns. "Sorry, sorry! We got lost."

The tour guide pushes through the congregation to examine the newcomers personally. "And where are your parents, boys?"

The truth—on opposite sides of the country—will hardly be to their satisfaction, so Andreas concocts a story they will want to hear. *"I got distracted and wandered off the path. My brother went after me. Our family came here to visit the bridge. Our parents are on the other side."* A mechanical voice inherently sounds authoritative.

The tour guide instinctively steps back at the sound of the tablet. "I, uh, imagine that happens a lot."

York looks between them. "What is that supposed to mean?"

Andreas knows what that is supposed to mean. The man who said it knows too: that because Andreas uses a tablet to talk, he must be such a burden to his parents, getting lost all the time. Never mind that he has maps on his tablet.

The man at least seems to have shame about the claim he has made. He is unable to maintain eye contact with them as he explains, "Well, this is a private group, so—"

"Oh, let them come!" a man, inexplicably in white robes, despite the weather, exclaims. "What's two more on this bridge?" He shuffles up to the tour guide, eyeing him critically. "Unless…"

"Th-That is very kind of you, Reverend!" the tour guide squeaks, trying to snuff out the seed of doubt before it can grow.

The man, Reverend, smiles at the brothers. The first thing Andreas notices is that the man's left eye is cloudy. The second thing Andreas notices is the great nickname potential for the name Reverend: "Rev," like a car, or—Actually, no, "End" is not a good nickname. So just that one. The third thing that Andreas notices is that he is mumbling about the safety of the bridge. *"If you are worried about safety, the bridge was re-done in 1999,"* the boy assures him. *"Now it's so safe that employees don't have to paint it from over the cliff!"*

Reverend hoots out a nervous laugh. "That's why I went into ministry! I work solely on God's green Earth!"

One of the members of Reverend's private group approaches cautiously. "Brother, you do not need to—"

"No!" Reverend barks. "I am facing my fear! It's just air! It's not *real!*"

York casts a worried glance at Andreas. Andreas returns it—because air *is* real.

"Sir—" York broaches. "—your fears *are* real. Because you feel them."

But Reverend stomps off to the front of the group again with a grim determination, like a person preparing to meet their maker.

* * *

It moves. No one told Andreas it would *move.*

That's not the truth. Andreas has read about the Mile High Swinging Bridge and knows the origin of its name. It is a mile high above sea level. Because it is a suspension bridge, it can swing. Each of those things sounded cool on paper—or on his tablet's screen. Combined, however, and in real life, it means that Andreas can't move.

He wants to. He wants to get off this bridge. But he's sweating. He's shaky. If he moves, he'll fall. He knows it. He knows this fact as surely as he knows the fact that the bridge is 228 feet long, and he'll be falling 5,280 feet to sea level.

He registers someone's voice: a celebration. He made it across! He registers someone else's voice: a question.

He recognizes his brother's voice. "Give us a minute!" A beat. "Or two!"

Then, he sees nothing but his brother's shirt. It's sky blue. He knew it. He's falling. He wants to scream, but it's being swallowed up by the air, which is all too real.

But something else is real too: the pressure of his brother's arms. His brother is holding him. His brother won't let him fall.

Wait, that isn't the sound of metal under his sneakers. That's dirt! *"No,"* his tablet says, completely unaffected by Andreas's hammering heart. *"I need to do it. I need to prove I can do it."* Reverend did it!

"You don't need to prove anything," York states. His voice sounds almost…mechanical, in how it doesn't leave any room for debate. It's comforting. "The bridge doesn't care! What I care about is if you *want* to cross the bridge."

And honestly? No. Not with so many people watching, understanding how much he can't do.

Also, he probably shouldn't start with the one of the highest suspension bridges in the country. Just a thought.

As Andreas shakes his head, he feels an unnatural amount of shade over him. He looks up, expecting to see, perhaps, the arms of the spruce trees stretched out, shielding him from the pitying tour group. Instead, he is face-to-face with a mob of fascinated faces teetering between recoil and study. York tells the tour group a boring story: that he will tell their parents to get them on their side of the bridge. Oh, that's right, they were lying. What if the people think they're lying about this too?

Slowly, those thoughts are crowded out by the continuous stream of York's thoughts. "You know I don't think any less of you because of this fear, right? Like how you don't think less of me because of my fears. I'm doing this for you like how you always let me get my vaccines first when we go to the doctor's office because I'm afraid of the needles."

Andreas doesn't like the needles either. He prefers doing his last, in the hopes that the doctors will forget about them. They haven't forgotten yet, but he keeps hoping.

"I'm doing this for you like how you go grab clothes near the mannequins when we go shopping because I'm afraid of the mannequins."

Okay, that one Andreas doesn't understand. The mannequins don't move. The mannequins don't hurt. He thinks they're weird, sure, but scary? No. He thinks they set a bad precedent, honestly. The mannequins can look all naked at the store, but people can't be naked! He leaves the changing room early *once* because they were supposed to be leaving already, and he gets banned from a whole store! A whole store full of mannequins, including the ones that look naked!

"FDR said the only thing to fear is fear itself. He's wrong. Fear is natural. Fear is okay. I, in fact, think the scariest thing is someone who has never known fear."

That certainly sounds good, but…*"Who is FDR?"* Andreas asks. He knows that FDR is famous because there are things on maps named after him, but—

York sputters as he rifles through his memories. "Someone I learned about in school," is the answer he lands on. "That's not his real name," he asserts. "His real name is longer."

Well, FDR is remembered enough to be taught in schools. He need not fear being forgotten. Andreas hopes that the group tour will forget him. He steals a look behind him and sees the stooped backs of interest defused.

CHAPTER 10

———

Huddled in their car, amongst the abandoned cereal boxes and forgotten wrappers, Andreas almost feels like he is back at home, snuggled up with his brother, hiding from their mother. Except he isn't hiding from a person. Andreas is hiding from a thing. A *bridge!* Bridges can't walk up and grab him!

"Sorry about that," York broaches, tucking his blanket around him, blocking his view of the floor. He must think he's pathetic: that if he lets Andreas think about the floor of the car for too long, he'll remember the floor of the bridge. Which wasn't a floor. Not really. A floor is solid. A floor is *safe.* That bridge wasn't safe. It can't walk up and grab him, but it can still hurt him. "I didn't know."

The problem is that Andreas didn't know either! He had seen pictures of mountains before, and they looked pretty, but it occurs to him that he had never bothered to look for pictures of the *drop.*

His hands are shaking. Andreas looks at his brother plaintively. What does he do? How does it *stop?*

York opens the car door. Andreas trains his gaze on his blanket. He doesn't think anyone else from the tour group followed them back, but he can't risk catching sight of any of them. They'd ask what happened. He doesn't have an answer to that question.

"May I touch you?" York has opened Andreas's door: the passenger-side door. He is standing in the doorway. If anyone is looking at them, they only see the wet spot on the butt cheek holder of York's shorts. Andreas thought the park benches would have dried out by then too.

This question, though? Andreas can answer this question. He nods silently. He's angry about how he jolts when York closes the door behind him. He's the one who insisted on leaving the park after his outburst! He can tell that York wanted to stay, and he's sure he could have found a dry park bench lower down to ride out the remaining shaking.

It's like York can hear the litany of apologies in Andreas's brain. His brother drowns them out with a litany of his own: "It's okay. I'm okay. You're okay. Let it out. Let it go. It's okay to feel not okay."

That is when the most not-okay thing happens: York's phone rings. The caller ID is like a burning dark star: *Mom.* York looks between the phone and Andreas desperately before stealing away, going to take the call behind their car.

Andreas curses his shakiness, but he forces his limbs into cooperation, clutching his tablet to his chest with both arms in case one gives out, stumbling out of the car, following the sound of their mother's shrill voice.

"I tried to warn you before, York: he's *terrified.*"

"Mom, it was awful. I don't know what to do to help!"

Andreas feels a shot of helplessness pierce his chest. *He* is giving their mother ammunition to bring York to his knees in submission. It's terrible. It's *terrifying.*

"You do know what to do to help. You're just afraid to do what must be done: bring your brother home."

Andreas knows what he must do. He swallows his shame to weaponize his shriek of terror. He hears York give a hasty apology to their mother, and then he hears the heavy footfalls of someone running with abandon. "Skippy, Skippy—" He continues his litany. "It's okay. I'm okay. You're okay. Let it out. Let it go. It's okay to feel not okay."

"I'm not okay," Andreas tells him. *"York, I'm terrified to go home. Mom says she knows how I feel but listen to me. Spending another six years with Mom is, to me, like spending six years on a bridge between the tallest mountains in Alaska."*

York's silence tells Andreas that he's said too much. "It's been a long day. Let's go to the nearest hotel." As they drive, the starry sky becomes less obscured by mountaintops and more obscured by the tips of trees.

As York slides out of the driver's side door, however, with the last few moments of car power before he retrieves the key, Andreas inputs their next destination into the GPS, cat's eye Venus staring down at him in approval. Andreas can only hope that *she* is looking down on him too. He can never forget what it felt like the second time he was too late to save a life. The memories of the first time, swirling around him like a storm, have reinvigorated his resolve.

* * *

"Did you input the directions to our next destination in the GPS last night?" Andreas nods. "Thanks!" York peers at the estimated time of arrival. "Four hours, huh? Yeah, that sounds about right."

Andreas doesn't press him about what it's about right for, but he tells his brother he can listen to his loud sad people on the way. To make up for the mountain. "You know I've been listening to my *bands*—" Andreas smiles at the strength of his brother's assertion that they're professionals, not loud sad people!—"on my headphones the whole time, right?"

York's giant, plastic, purple headphones are hard to miss, nor is the wire trailing down his face to his phone. "I'll take you up on your offer regardless! You set the volume, though, okay?"

It's a compromise. It's what co-existence is based on. And they need to cooperate. Because they're going to conquer this challenge! *"Fine, I'll cooperate. We're going to conquer this drive!"*

Andreas's tongue pokes out of his mouth as he inputs the word "conquer" into his tablet in an echo. He extends the "o" and adds a space after the first two letters to accentuate the false flag prefix. *"Co-nquer?"*

His brother laughs. "How many times did you need to adjust the spacing to make the tablet make that one work?"

Too many. Luckily, his brother didn't hear most of the attempts through the loud sad people.

On one of the loud sad albums, there is a "secret track." It's called a "secret track" because the thirty seconds of song is a secret: one that they don't know about until York is about to skip ahead to the next song. "Oh, right. This song! I guess I forgot about it."

York's phone's buzzing drowns out the thirty-second secret song. Andreas reads the name on the screen. *"It's her,"* he tells him.

York wisely decides to pull over. He picks up the phone and immediately clicks the speaker button. "Hello, Mom."

"Did you make your decision?"

Andreas looks at York, waiting for his judgment, as unblinking as cat's eye Venus. "Yes," York answers.

"When will you be home?"

"That's not the decision I made."

Their mother's voice snaps like saccharine caramel. "How close are you to New York?"

It's starting to feel like an interrogation. Andreas silently types on his tablet and presents his counter-question to his brother. York nods and questions, "Why are you so fixated on New York?"

"Because I know you're going to see him. I heard you talking to your father on the phone. When you see him, I want to get on the phone with him."

Andreas starts typing out another question, but York beats him to it. "Why are you so sure that we're going to see Dad?"

"Because you just told me!" she accuses. "And I keep the letters he sends you on your birthdays! I know he told you to look at colleges in New York!"

Andreas quirks a brow at the phone. Well, yes, their father said that once. In a letter. A year ago. But does she not remember that York has been meeting with Coach Diego once a week for a year to talk about colleges? Also, York only read that letter once before their mother demanded it for her archive—not that either of them had letters interesting enough to warrant reading more than once. Andreas has been taking pictures of his to test a theory he had. "Hello, boy! I can't believe that you are seven, eight, nine, ten, eleven, twelve years old! How is school? Are you learning anything?" Andreas's birthday may only come once a year, but does his father really think he doesn't remember each of his previous birthdays?

York hasn't let Andreas take pictures of his letters, but Andreas has seen that they follow a similar formula.

"Why can't you just call Dad?" York offers. "He gave me his new number on one of the cards, so you must have it."

Their mother shuts down his suggestion. "Because he doesn't want to talk to me."

Then why do you assume we want to talk to you? York is more polite than Andreas is, though, because he says, "We'll talk to Dad about talking to you when we see him then, okay?"

Apparently, that is okay. No more questions now that she can't accuse them of going in the wrong direction.

The brothers wait in tense silence for their mother to call them back, having decided she is not actually okay with York having the last word. When it doesn't happen, though, York says, "Well, then. Back to the music?"

* * *

As they enter the city limits of Raleigh, the forests of Grandfather Mountain now fully receded into flat shoreline, Andreas requests that they turn the music off. Now, both need to be attentive to directions. "So where are we, Skippy?"

"Raleigh," he answers. Ooh, there's a raleighflorist.com? Convenient! For Gingerbread House Florist & Gifts, that is. The competition? Not so much.

"Raleigh?" his brother yelps. Without the GPS' prompting, he makes a U-turn! "I'm sorry, Skippy, but we have to go somewhere else. Charlotte is a big city in North Carolina if that's what you want!"

But Charlotte is back two and a half hours to the west! More importantly, Charlotte *wasn't* her name. Andreas tells his brother neither of these things, though. Instead, he begins to keen.

York panics at his brother's crying. "I'm sorry! What do you want to do in Raleigh? We can do it somewhere else!" He's pulling over. "You look at the map. I'll look at the GPS. North Carolina is a big state. Heck, there are still so many states north of here on our trip to New York!"

There is only one place in the whole world where he can let her go, though. Andreas wraps his arms around himself and starts squeezing away the urge to peel at his face. He realizes that he's terrified of forgetting her before he can honor her. He did right by Atlas by saving Stormy. He's not under any delusions that he'll save some other girl's life, thereby balancing out the fact that he didn't stop her from taking her own... He sobs. So much he can't do. Like understanding. Why did Raleigh do it?

His brother's hands are taking his hands away from his face. Andreas's gaze drifts out toward the window. Raleigh Durham International Airport is right next to them. The florist isn't far, and it's just south of Falls Lake. So...twenty minutes away. He knows he doesn't have his own car, but that doesn't stop people. People use an app. He'll have to download one on his tablet, but he'll make it work. He knows it's traditional to use the ocean to give mourning flowers to, but her name wasn't Ocean. No, it needs to happen in Raleigh.

"—ippy!" The undercurrent of noise rolls into the foreground. "I'll tell you why. I'll tell you why we can't go to Raleigh." The boy yanks his hands away and sits on them. For safety. His older brother sighs, and the words come out of him like a sacred confession: "Her little brother's name is Gage."

Raleigh's little brother? No, that can't be right! She was an only child, and what she wanted was an older brother. Furthermore, York never got to meet Raleigh. They would have been friends.

York isn't hiding from a friend, though, is he? Andreas's fingers stab at the tablet. *"What does any little brother other than me have to do with anything?"*

"Gage is how we met, not that he's the one who's here, but—" Well, that at least confirms to Andreas that they are not, in fact, talking about the same person. But who *is* York talking about? It can't be as important as what he needs to do, since York never mentioned this person before. The boy looks at his brother. There is an unusual amount of will in his eyes. Normally, Andreas would be proud at such a development, but not when it gets in the way of his own will. Luckily, he knows whose will is stronger. Andreas hardens his gaze into a glare.

And the willful walls around his brother crumble. "Never mind," York declares. "Raleigh is a big city, isn't it?"

"404,068 people," Andreas quotes from the 2010 census.

His brother seizes on his confidence. "And she's one person! And I know which school she's in!" His hands grip the steering wheel. The knuckles go white, but he does not cave to sweaty palms. "Put in the address."

* * *

Andreas hadn't expected to see flowers outside!

Outside the cabinets, that is. Of course, he expects to see flowers *outside*. More than having flowers merely outside the cabinets, though, Gingerbread House Florist & Gifts has plants growing on the walls! They don't appear to have flowered yet, and honestly, that might be a good thing. He's walked around the entire store—the whole room—and he hasn't seen a ladder tall enough to get the woman behind the counter stable under them. He's taller than the woman, so he could offer his services, but he's not getting on a ladder. Not after Grandfather Mountain. He doesn't trust North Carolina heights.

He'll try a California ladder when he gets back.

"Howdy, sugar! You've been looking around for a while! Can Ah help you with your decisions?" He figures that most of her customers can ask the person they're getting the flowers for for help, but that isn't an option for him. This is a woman in Raleigh. She has a connection to the girl named Raleigh in that way. He nods.

What flowers do you get for the dead? he inquires.

"Oh, my!" the florist gasps. "Ah am sorry for your loss! Lord have mercy!" She waves her hand around. He hastily copies her. Maybe she's pointing to the flowers he needs?

She ends up not just pointing to the flowers but personally retrieving them. "I became a florist to punctuate the happy occasions," she chatters. "Funeral arrangements are my *least* favorite part of my job!"

Funeral, yes. It will be a private funeral. She explains the basket of flowers to him. "These here are lilies. They represent innocence, like Adam and Eve, God rest their souls!"

Andreas is sorry for her loss. Losing one friend is hard enough, never mind two. He wonders how Adam and Eve and the florist met.

"Carnations of many colors are used as sympathy flowers. I think pink ones work best for this arrangement, though. They stand for the memories you and the others have of this poor lamb."

There are funerals for animals? He will have to remember that! He thinks he has honored Atlas, but, after rescuing

Stormy, he realizes that he misses having a cat. He thinks York will agree to having another cat when they're living on their own. York can help him plan the cat's funeral when the time comes. They'll keep this cat away from the road, so it will be a long time. He knows York was sad after Atlas's murder too, even though he didn't go to a support group after it. Now that Andreas thinks about it, maybe that is because York did not scratch his cheek after Atlas's murder as if that means that his brother did not need support.

"—and these are…"

Oh. Andreas knows those. *"Red roses,"* he utters. *"For love."*

The woman nods. "I think we all know and love roses! Red roses are good for more than just romance. They also express respect for the dearly departed and highlight the courage it takes to grieve." She takes in a whiff of the arrangement. "It also completes the color spectrum Ah'm aiming for here! White and red make pink! In order to remember a person, we must acknowledge both the innocence of life and the courage of continuing to live. After all, to end a life, granted to us by our Heavenly Father, is a sin!"

Andreas thinks about how black the heart of Atlas's murderer is. Still, when he thinks about Raleigh, he cannot reconcile the evil of killing with the kindness she showed him.

* * *

The kindness began at that first meeting, Andreas remembers. He was ten years old. The cat he rescued as a kitten had died in his arms, and all everyone seemed to talk about was his cheek.

Apparently, that was why he was at that meeting: his cheek. "These people will help you get better," his mother had told him. No, ordered him—as if there was no alternative.

Andreas was used to orders. In a way, they comforted him. If he did what these people told him to do, he'd stop waking up and expecting to see Atlas pawing at his cheek. As he entered, he was rubbing his scarred cheek protectively.

On one hand, his mother wasn't there to introduce him—"This is Andreas, and he doesn't understand." On the other hand, his mother had taken his tablet away.

She said he needed to pay attention.

Well, how was he supposed to pay attention if he was stuck as a stranger to these people? These people couldn't help him if they didn't know him!

But then one of the strangers called out to him. "You can sit next to me!"

She didn't even know him—couldn't know him, even—and still, she invited him in. There were many things Andreas learned about her that first day: She loved the ocean, her favorite color was purple, and she was lactose intolerant. In that order. Yes, there was her short, curly, black hair and her brown skin, and there was that she was the only one in the room with black hair and brown skin, and the standard name and age—Raleigh and eleven—but those were never things she talked about. Because those things were announced to them.

Announced through the lady with the tie-dye skirt. Announced through the eyes. It was the lady's mouth, and it was their eyes, but it was still orders. Orders to decide that names and age and skin were important, whereas the things that cause smiles aren't.

Raleigh didn't smile that first day, but even so, Andreas imagined it.

* * *

For the whole first week, Raleigh only learned things that didn't matter about him. The standard name and age—Andreas and ten. His short, blond hair and his pale skin and his blue eyes. And the scar on his cheek.

But at the end of the first week, a good report—"Andy appears to be attentive," and, really, the program director couldn't have been that attentive herself if she didn't figure out his name yet, even though saying their names and ages was how they began every session—earned him back his voice.

The first thing Andreas told Raleigh after that first class, with his own voice, was that he loved the ocean too. "I like the waves," he explained. "It's noise, but it's good noise. It's always there. Like…" he said hopefully. "Like a friend."

Raleigh's dark eyes were bright. "There are friends in the ocean too!" she exclaimed.

Andreas's brow furrowed in confusion. "People don't live in the ocean."

"Better than people!"

Andreas had never met anyone so willing to tell the truth before.

* * *

Raleigh loved the ocean. Raleigh also loved to talk about the friends in the ocean.

"The earliest creatures that we think are fish—" She pulled at her t-shirt of neon-colored fish, kicking her feet, although they dragged across the ground from where she sat on the edge of the flower bed outside the church where the meetings were held. "—came out during the Cambrian Period."

Andreas pondered the statement from where he sat on the steps of the church, not having trusted his ability not to fall

from the flowerbed onto the asphalt of the church parking lot.
"When was the Cambrian Period?"

Raleigh blinked rapidly before recovering. "Why, when there was Cambria, duh!"

Andreas considered the facts he learned in school. The pre-historic period was before there was history. The Great Depression period was when there was the Great Depression. Yes, the facts checked out.

"Anyway, who cares about the Cambrian Period?" she insisted. "That was a long time ago! Blue whales, on the other hand, exist now, and they're the—"

"Wait, you were just talking about fish," *he pointed out.* "So that applies to the whale too!"

Raleigh suddenly flung herself off and away from the flowerbed, landing in front of him. "Whales are not fish!" she roared. "Whales are marine mammals!"

From the fish to the whales, no marine animal—mammal or otherwise—was too small or too large for Raleigh to talk about.

"Despite being called killer whales, the Orcinus orca—*or just orca—is not a whale," she told him the day after his mistake. "It's a dolphin! And whales are…"*

"…Mammals," *Andreas supplied. Really, he made that mistake once. Once!*

Raleigh smiled when she talked about marine animals. And when she told him whales are mammals, not fish. And despite being told whales are mammals, not fish, Andreas too smiled.

* * *

Raleigh did not smile about most things. Andreas found that refreshing. She only smiled about things that really made her happy. Andreas thought that was a strength.

Smiling about things that don't make you happy only allows for people to keep giving you things that don't make you happy.

One meeting, they were asked what they looked forward to in the future.

Aiko, twelve, said she was looking forward to the Japanese New Year celebrations. Zoe, eleven, said she was looking forward to going to a new movie with her girlfriend. Little Ferdinand, the youngest of the group at age nine, said he couldn't wait for his dog to have her puppies!

Raleigh didn't smile during the activity. She also didn't say anything.

Andreas didn't say anything either, even when he had his tablet. The lady with the tie-dye skirt said they could talk about one thing. One thing! How could he narrow it down? There was high school—he could finally understand what York is talking about! There were new movies, including one York was excited for. There were adorable cat videos. He'd make York watch at least one of them, mark his words! And, most of all, there was living with York. One more year, and his brother would be an adult.

* * *

Andreas finally worked up the courage to ask the question. "Why is your favorite color purple? Why isn't it blue, like the ocean?"

"The ocean isn't blue!" she shouted, pulling at her blue skirt as if to correct him. "Water is clear!"

"Why isn't it clear, then?" *he pressed.*

"Because purple changed my life." *She looked down at his tablet.* "You can look up pictures, right? Look up Silk Soy Milk."

It's easy enough to find: a purple carton. "Milk changed your life?"

"Not-cow-milk milk changed my life." *She leaned in conspiratorially.* "Can you imagine cramping every morning after your morning milk and cereal?"

Andreas didn't eat cereal with milk, but he had an imagination, and he imagined it to be awful.

* * *

They did another round of the "What do you look forward to in the future?" activity. When the lady in the tie-dye skirt said that, this time, everyone would need to answer the question, Raleigh went pale.

And as the question got closer to her, rising like a wave, Raleigh curled in on herself, as if steeling herself to try to float once the wave hit. The question crested, and all of a sudden, Raleigh unfurled.

Andreas watched her bolt to the bathroom. He heard a wet sound.

Andreas felt the bile in his mouth too, but he choked it down and waited outside the bathroom for her to emerge. He convinced the lady in the tie-dye skirt that Raleigh was sick.

Andreas waited outside with Raleigh for her mom—mom, not mother*—to pick her up. Fresh air was supposed to be good for sick people, right? But Andreas watched her fold over herself again.*

Andreas couldn't see the wave she was bracing for.

* * *

The next day, Raleigh asked him a question. Her voice rose like a wave. "How do you answer that question?" she demanded, tears in her eyes. "How do you answer a question about the future, about what you want to do there?" She squeezed her eyes, trying to force her tears back in, but, instead, they trickled out. "How do you talk about the future like it's something you can see?"

"It's hard," *Andreas admitted.* "Because there are so many answers. Things you want to get to, things you want to get away from...I picked high school because my brother talks about it a lot."

"Your brother..." she murmured. "His name is York, right? I wish I had a sibling."

"It's not always easy," *he admitted.* "He's always listening to loud, sad music that I hate—"

She cut him off. "But he's always there, isn't he? It's just me and Mom. Most of the time, I'm alone. I don't like it."

"You're not alone!" *Andreas was quick to type, even allowing some typos to get through.* "I'm with you!"

She laughed then, but it wasn't a happy laugh. "Andreas, you don't belong here."

He remembered feeling defensive then. No, he was picked to come here! Because he needed to get better! He wasn't going to let Raleigh be alone again that easily!

But the threat remained. If the lady with the tie-dye skirt decided that he didn't belong, then she would tell his mother, and then he would be gone.

So, Raleigh needed to not be alone, even if he wasn't there.

She needed something that she could do on her own...but not alone. Andreas attacked the puzzle with gusto. It wasn't enough to find something that Raleigh could do. It needed to be something that she wanted *to do!*

He reviewed the information: She loved the ocean, her favorite color was purple, and she was lactose intolerant. In that order.

"That's it!" Andreas exclaimed one day when they were paired up to do a writing exercise. "You can *be with your friends in the ocean!"*

"I've thought of that," Raleigh muttered. "I love the ocean, but...I hate sand. It's...It's a feeling. Like something crawling in between my fingers and toes."

Andreas had never met someone who admitted to that truth before. "Okay, no sand. We'll figure something else out."

"There isn't anything to figure out. Every ocean has sand."

* * *

Andreas researched that question: Does every ocean have sand? He discovered salty oceans. He discovered rocky oceans. He even discovered frozen oceans, but the frozen oceans were where there were no people, and that was the opposite *of what was needed!*

Yes, there was water without sand, but that was water in bathtubs and pools. No friends in there. No non-human friends, anyway. No friends that could be trusted to stay.

Inspiration struck in an unlikely place: on the way to one of his brain doctors' appointments. Psychologist? Psychiatrist? One of those. "They're opening a new aquarium?" his mother had uttered.

Andreas studied the sign. He looked up the website. And there they were: fish and whales and Orcinus orca. *All in one place. And not a speck of sand to be found.*

Andreas burst into the next meeting with a question, but Raleigh wasn't there to answer it.

* * *

He learned about what Raleigh's future had turned into in the hallway, when the lady with the tie-dye skirt was ushering his mother to a woman with short, curly, black hair and brown skin, in a long-sleeved black dress. The sleeves had smear marks that shone. The stranger rubbed her nose against her sleeve as his mother approached. "I wanted to talk to you. I know they were friends."

Andreas expected his mother to brush her off—rubbing your nose on your clothes was the peak of rudeness to her, after all—but, instead, she took the other woman's hand, clasping it between two of hers. He watched his mother open her mouth, but no words came out.

"You don't have to say anything," the other woman murmured. "There are no words. Except...Don't tell yourself that your boy can't do it. That's what I thought too, but...My Raleigh is gone now."

Andreas felt like he had been dunked in a freezing ocean, and he was left gasping for breath. Raleigh was gone, and not "gone" as in "moved to a different school." Raleigh was gone, as in "she would never be able to answer his question."

Or be with her friends in the ocean.

He watched as her mom—mom, not mother—sobbed and buried her face in his mother's shoulder, and his mother was flash-frozen to the spot, holding her breath, as if afraid that the other woman would blow away. Raleigh would never be with her mom either. Did she think her mom would just smile and wave as she left?

Did she think he would just be okay with her leaving?

She must have not known. He wasn't able to tell her, even with his voice, how important it was that she stayed.

Andreas howled and hurled the useless vessel of useless words at the floor.

Both his mother and the lady with the tie-dye skirt came running from further into the hallway, where he was frozen to the doorway of the meeting room, and in that moment, Andreas realized the alternative his mother had seen.

It was no alternative for him. He wouldn't be leaving York alone. And never mind York. What about his *future? He couldn't leave his future alone! If not him, who will make his dreams come true?*

He picked up his tablet, checking to make sure he had not gone away in his rage. He touched the scar on his cheek with his right hand. He ran his left index finger over the scar on the tablet's screen. Raleigh's memory, too, would never leave him.

* * *

No, the color of Raleigh's heart is purple. Red for love—for the ocean, for the friends inside it, and maybe for a friend outside it—mixed with blue for sadness. Because despite being surrounded by ocean and having someone sitting next to her every meeting, she still felt alone.

CHAPTER 11

———

Andreas thanks the florist for her time and pays for her services. He walks out with a flower-filled basket and deposits it on his lap. As he begins to input the directions to Falls Lake, though, York is peering out the window, nervously trilling to himself. Andreas asks him about it.

"I'm just hungry."

If his brother were really hungry, he'd just get food. He has no qualms about eating at weird times. That being said, it isn't a weird time to get lunch. Andreas looks up nearby restaurants. He is not going to a mall, thank you very much. Al Baraka Market and Grill looks like a good place to get something quick.

He submits the address. "Hillsborough Street?" York yelps.

"*What's wrong with Hillsborough Street?*"

"Nothing, nothing!" Ah, yes, because his brother normally panics at street names.

And, honestly, Andreas is panicking about his driving. Every time he sees a blonde woman on the street, he jerks his head away. But none of the women are looking at them!

"Eyes on the road!" Andreas yells, turning his tablet up to maximum volume, even though the volume hurts, because a car crash would hurt worse!

The worst of it is when they are at a red light, and a convertible pulls up next to them. The young women are all only a little bit older than York, so maybe it's legal for them to be drinking, but if Andreas can smell it on their breaths, they really shouldn't be driving. Thankfully, only one of them is blonde, but, of course, she is the one to lean out the passenger side window and drawl, "Hey, cutie."

Normally, York doesn't even try to skirt through yellow lights. At that comment, though, he speeds past the red light.

By some miracle, they pull into Al Baraka Market and Grill safely. Andreas lets his brother eat in silence because he can tell that his brother is actually not very hungry, which isn't a good sign at all, but the worst sign is the truth: York's behavior is putting them in danger. So, Andreas must ask: *"Who are you looking for?"*

"No one, okay?" York snaps. "No one!"

His brother is a terrible liar. No one looking for no one works so hard to not look at anyone. Looking for no one is easy. Looking for someone—or rather, looking to not be seen by someone—is difficult. But who is York trying to avoid so much? Enough that he is putting their safety at risk? Something Andreas does understand pokes through the shaking earth of his frustration: York cares about their safety, so he must not be aware of how unsafe he is being. From the subject of safety, maybe they can move toward the source of York's flightiness.

"The way you're driving right now is unsafe," the pre-teen informs him.

York's puffed-out chest deflates, and he curls his arms around himself, all the hot, pent-up anger hardening into guilt. For his part, Andreas is angry at himself. No, guilt won't help them! He can re-direct anger, but guilt is hard to move. Especially since he doesn't know what the problem is!

"It's summer."

Andreas nods cautiously. Is the heat the problem? He can get his brother some water. They can go by the water, up toward Falls Lake...

"School's out for summer," York breathes reverently.

Well, yes, obviously. Their mother was reluctant enough to allow them to go on the road trip that she *promised* they could go on when they had nothing to do. She would have used all of her power to prevent them from leaving school— never mind that York is smart and Andreas doesn't learn anything at school except how important sitting still is.

"She won't be there." York's head whips toward him, so quickly that Andreas swears he hears something in the neck crack. His green eyes glinting with desperation, York makes a request of his brother: "Can you look up an address?"

"*What address?*" Andreas asks.

The answer he gets is, "Meredith College."

The boy looks up from his tablet, then looks across the street. "*You mean* that *Meredith College?*"

At York's confusion, Andreas shows him the directions. "Oh," he utters. "It's that close? I thought there would be a gate or something—"

A quick dig through the college website reveals that there is a "gatehouse" farther down the Hillsborough Street entrance. Andreas relays this information to his brother.

"What's a gatehouse?" York tries.

Andreas shrugs because that's not the important question, now is it? The important question is, *"Do you want to find out?"*

* * *

The gatehouse is a very small house. It barely seems to fit the police officer inside of it. As they walk along the road, they expect for her to stop them, but she stops neither them nor the apparent touring family group exiting on the other side of the street. Andreas returns to the college website. It claims that the officers only regulate travel beyond normal business hours and only intervene when they spot "suspicious activity."

Neither of them trusts what they read on the internet, though. Somehow, they are always "suspicious."

Once they clear the officer's line of sight, however, Andreas cannot deny the spring in his step. They're in a *college!* The buildings are big and brick, and the people are brainy! He knows his brother will fit right in! *"Does this college look like yours?"* Andreas asks him.

"I mean, I guess so? Don't all colleges look alike?"

Andreas stops jumping. *"You haven't seen your college yet?"* he asks in disbelief.

York cocks his head at him. "Do you remember me leaving with Mom alone anytime this year?"

Andreas concedes the point. When they get to the Northeast, they'll fix that! They'll visit York's college—the best college—without their mother breathing down their necks! Andreas resumes watching the campus with renewed vigor. He needs to be ready to compare and contrast.

Meredith College's main buildings are marked by white pillars, against the rest of their brown brick exterior.

Sometimes, the trees are carefully trimmed back so as not to obscure their entrances, but there are a few buildings where the trees have gained dominance. Andreas prefers these buildings. Between the brown bark of the trees and the brown brick of the building, he can pretend that he's entering the trees themselves: an illusion that is shattered when the interior of the building is decidedly not brown—he can tell that even when peering through the windows—but he bets that if he opens the windows, the buildings could end up *smelling* like trees. Trees! Who knew The East had so many trees?

Wait, and water? It makes sense—so many trees need to drink from somewhere—but a part of Andreas still doesn't believe it when the college's website declares that the campus has a lake!

"Can we go to Meredith Lake?" Andreas asks York. *"It looks like we can get there through the theater!"*

They start heading back toward the Hillsborough Street entrance, where they came from. As they reach the hill that the campus map says is near the theater, Andreas hops in excitement.

The theater isn't at the bottom of the hill! It *is* the hill! The stone seats jut out in a natural slope, and he's *sure* that the water can be used for special effects! *"It looks ancient!"* Andreas cries.

"That's what it's supposed to look like," York concedes, shrugging. "I don't know why so many colleges are obsessed with these things, Skippy. Wooden chairs are uncomfortable enough to sit in—never mind slabs of stone!"

The boy twirls around. *"There are more of these hill-the-aters?"* At his brother's lukewarm nod, Andreas harrumphs and plants himself on the top row of the stone seats.

Andreas realizes that they are, in fact, uncomfortable. *"I'm sure they give people pillows,"* Andreas reasons. With the college's logo on them too! Meredith College sells a lot of things with their logo on them: blankets, umbrellas, water bottles...

Andreas explains his idea to his brother as they descend, but York isn't convinced. "Look how many seats there are! How many pillows would that be? College pillows can't be that popular!"

Oh, but the evidence to the contrary is all around them! Pillows aren't expensive but the big brick buildings are! Where did all that money come from? People buying things! People buying applications! People buying classes! People buying textbooks!

And, yes, Andreas tells York as they climb up the stairs to exit the hill-theater, people buying things from the campus gift shop. It's clearly popular! He sees a young woman with long, blond hair coming down the stairs from Jones Hall, the building directly across from them, her dark blue scuffed jean shorts above her knees, showing tanned legs. Andreas will admit that the maroon of the Meredith College t-shirt skulks off the potential for fuzzy lighting and swelling music. He's never seen a Meredith College t-shirt on a person in a movie.

Andreas does recognize the part, however, where the woman trots over to begin the scene. "Well, aren't I lucky to see you, Lucky?"

Andreas stifles the initial flare of anger at the word. He's *not* lucky. He's not lucky to be in "easy classes." He's not lucky to have a tablet. He's not lucky to have someone who loves him *despite.* Because there's always "despite."

Despite his instinctive reaction, however, the woman is not talking to him. Andreas looks behind him. York is backing up, creeping back down the stairs, toward the lake. Scared.

Andreas doesn't hold his anger back. He runs down the rest of the stairs to stand before the woman his brother was looking for, who looks at York like a relic of the past.

The fear in his brother is tangible as he stutters out, "G-G-Geneva." It's tangible as the name echoes under his breath.

"Why don't you come to my room, Lucky? We can catch up—"

He cuts her off with, "I'm saying yes this time!"

Well, Andreas is saying no. *"Who are you?"* he demands.

Geneva ruffles Andreas's hair as she strides past him. "Oh, you're right, Lucky, he *is* a sweetheart." Andreas steps out of her grip, swerving to confront his brother. Why does she know him if he doesn't know her?

He remembers York's explanation: *"Gage is how we met."* Did they talk about their little brothers? But why? York is on the soccer team. They could have shared classes together. Did York even meet Gage? Or did he and Geneva just trade cryptic tips about their little brothers?

Andreas doesn't know what's going on, but he does know one thing: *"I'm coming with you."* York looks petrified, and, yes, Andreas knows that this is stranger danger, but if they're going to face danger, it's better that they do it together.

It would have been better if York said no to coming with her, but as Geneva wraps her hand in his brother's and lays her fingernails over his wrist, Andreas knows that she has power over him.

Sometimes, it's impossible to say no to someone who has power over you.

* * *

She takes them to a building called Heilman. York's eyes widen with hope as she tugs at the door to no avail, but she tuts at herself before swiftly dialing a phone number on her cell phone. "Girls?" she chirps. "You know how I was just telling a story about a guy I dated in high school?"

Andreas yelps in shock. As he turns to his brother, though, he does not see the red cheeks of love but the white face of fear.

"Well, guess who just showed up?...I know, right! Lucky! Let us in."

A trio of young women, all wearing soccer jerseys, smush their faces against the windows. Andreas can hear them squealing already. They are outnumbered two to one. He presses against his brother, so they can't get separated.

The three soccer players spill out of Heilman Hall. "Oh my gosh! You didn't tell us he has a *brother!*"

York throws an arm out in front of Andreas. "He is twelve years old."

"He's so *tall!*" the shortest one says. She is two inches taller than Andreas. The same height as York.

The tallest one takes note of this. "Shame he's not getting much taller."

"We'll see," Geneva cuts in. "Come on, Lucky. You're a freshman now, right? You need to see what upperclassmen dorms can look like!" She pulls him inside.

* * *

Andreas had been excited to see a sampling of the college experience, since he knows he's not going to college himself. Something about his "numbers" not being high enough. He knows York worked hard on many tests to get his own numbers high enough. Now, though, all he can see is the terror on his brother's face. York does not dare turn his back on Geneva. In fact, as soon as they enter her room, he slams his back against the wall and pulls Andreas to it too! Against the wall, Andreas marvels at a girl's room. It looks remarkably similar to York's room, at least when he isn't storing his maps in there. There is a collection of soccer jerseys, steadily increasing in size, along each bed, with the exception of one, which has a collection of cheerleading uniforms instead. Framing the door is a collection of posters featuring people with guitars—they may not be *York's* loud, sad people with guitars, but they are loud, sad people, nevertheless.

Andreas wrenches his hand from his brother's clammy grip. He doesn't know why York is afraid of this woman, but he is not scared of her! *"What do you want?"* he roars.

The one who hasn't said anything yet, the medium-sized soccer player, examines his tablet. "How old is that iPad? You need to get a new one." Her comment precipitates a wave of agreement from the other three women, who unanimously decide that it is lame.

"As if I asked for your opinion!" Andreas exclaims. *"Now—"*

The medium-sized soccer player crosses her arms at him. "Then why don't you ask?"

"I'll repeat my question if you didn't understand! What do you—"

Geneva waves her friend down. "Ah, it's coming back to me! You told me that he can't talk, didn't you, Lucky?"

Andreas doesn't make the mistake of turning his back on her, but he doesn't let that revelation go by without confronting York: *"Why did you talk to someone you don't like about me?"*

Because that's the crux of it: York wasn't looking for someone he liked.

"Oh, that's not true," Geneva coos. "You told me you loved me, that night at the party." She turns to her friends and chatters on about the end-of-school-year bash the soccer team was throwing, "Oh, what was it, four summers ago? Or was it three?"

All Andreas can hear, though, is York's soft, "Did I?"

The boy slides back to the wall. He sets the volume on his tablet as low as he can before he broaches the subject: *"You need to tell me what happened."* All Andreas knows is that he asked when York came home, and York didn't answer. Because he was scared. Andreas thought, at the time, that York was scared about their mother finding out about the party, but now...

"I don't remember what happened," his brother confesses. York looks up furtively and shrinks when he realizes, even in their "private" corner, four sets of eyes are on them. "Not a lot of it. I only went to the party because the team told me I needed to, and while I don't really like soccer, I liked doing *something* to *fit in*, so I went." He shakes his head. "But I regretted it immediately. It was so loud, and there were so many people that someone was always touching me...Touching me..." As his quavering voice forces an echo, the three soccer players peer over Geneva's shoulders. York closes his eyes at their inspection. "And then Geneva was there. She'd gotten me something to drink. Drink. That was nice of her. Nice of her. And then it gets fuzzy. Fuzzy. I felt weird. Weird. She told me she was going to take me somewhere quiet. Quiet. It was someone's bedroom. Bedroom. And then we..."

Andreas has seen the teen drama movies, but he doesn't see any fuzzy lighting or swelling music in that scene. In fact, he sees the blue and red of police sirens.

Andreas looks at Geneva anew. She is a car, making her brother into roadkill: something to be pitied, something to be conquered. And then something to be forgotten.

Geneva does not forget to tell her friends *her* side of the story. "He was so happy to follow me to the bedroom… He says he doesn't like touching, but that's not what I found out… Actions speak louder than words, you know." And Geneva's story may have more details, but none of its scenes have anything of real import. She breezes over them with all the indifference of tires on the road.

Andreas turns to his brother. *"If we're going to get out of here, I'm going to need your help."* The young man nods numbly. Now he needs to develop a plan. *Come on, Skippy, think!*

This isn't a scene of fuzzy lighting and swelling music, but he has seen this scene before! In the high school movies! They were such stressful movies, full of leering and jeering. If he wants to watch people gossip and ostracize him, he can pay attention at school. York, however, defended the teen dramas as informative. He even went so far as to call them *documentaries!*

But what information did they provide? Cars are freedom, finals are awful, popular people have power, and underclassmen are uncool. Wait, rewind! How many summers ago did Geneva say this party was? Three? If this party took place three years ago, then his brother had just completed sophomore year, since he repeated ninth grade. He was an uncool underclassman!

And even if his math is wrong, the fact that York is an underclassman isn't wrong now!

"That's so lame," Andreas says, mimicking the character Geneva would be.

"What's so lame?" the shortest soccer player echoes.

He knows this scene: the climax, where the clique turns and kicks someone out. *"He's an* underclassman," Andreas huffs. *"An underclassman who doesn't even like you!"*

The soccer players analyze the brothers like they are on the roster for the other team. They frown at the stats. "Geneva," the medium-sized girl says. "The brother can't even *talk*."

Andreas shoots a look at his brother. Come on, he needs to be lame right *now!* York begins repeating the word under his breath. No, the word *lame* isn't lame! He's lame because he's an underclassman! Do an underclassman thing! Ask for a ride! Because he doesn't have a car!

But he *does* have a car! The plan is falling apart. Andreas growls in frustration.

The soccer players take a step back. Andreas instinctively steps back too, toward his brother. He didn't mean to scare them!

"Let them go," the medium-sized girl demands, locking gazes with Geneva. "Then leave."

"What?" Geneva yelps. "Why do I need to leave?"

"Because Geneva!" the leader shouts back. "If he can't remember it, he couldn't have liked it!" She thrusts an arm out toward York. "We're not stupid. It's *obvious* he didn't like what you did."

Andreas jolts at the sound of the door screeching. The other two soccer players have opened it. It's like the rush of air streaming in from a window. Freedom awaits. Andreas locks arms with his brother, and they break out.

* * *

They do not speak again until they arrive at Falls Lake. In the fresh air, it is easy to feel like they were never trapped. As Andreas looks over at his brother, though, he realizes that he has been chained down for a long time.

"It's more than lame." York starts at the sound of the tablet. *"All I was thinking about was how to get us out of there, but I should have been thinking about how we should get out of there. If that makes sense?"*

"That felt wrong," York admits.

"That's because it was *wrong! That's the word for it! Not* lame! *I was wrong to do that! To push you!"* Andreas realizes an advantage of a mechanical voice: He can speak while he cries. *"How could I have done that? It's supposed to be us against the world."* He didn't see that his brother was scared when he came back from the party, the same way he didn't see that Raleigh was—

"May I touch you?" Andreas feels his head wobbling as he presses his face against his brother's shirt. "If you were wrong, then so was I. I should have told you—"

Andreas cuts him off. *"You are under no obligation to re-live your fear just so I can understand it. Your fears are real because you feel them."* York smiles at his own words being reflected back at him. *"Your fears are the truth regardless of who else knows, and the truth always wins over lies."*

His brother frowns. "Here's the thing…I did love her back then. As more than a friend. I have a little brother who can't talk. She has a little brother who can't walk. I thought she would understand." He shakes his head. "I guess that shows how much I understand, huh?"

So much we can't do, the boy muses. But Andreas can do this. *"Is you loving her the truth now?"*

"No," York states definitively. "No, it's not." Andreas nods. York agreed to see Geneva because he was forced to. Because of him. And because he had experienced the consequences of saying no to her.

"*Then it* is *the truth.*" And the other women learned that truth at least.

CHAPTER 12

——

York parallel-parks on Tomilson Avenue in The Bronx, too worn out from the battle to get into New York City to care that he is clipping the curb. Too tired to wait for the click of a locked door as he trudges toward the sidewalk. Andreas, wanting to avert disaster, scrambles to slam the driver-side door shut, clutching the car keys in his hands. He clicks the lock button twice, just to make sure.

"Thanks, Skippy," York murmurs. He stifles a yawn as they get onto their father's stoop: a gray, plantless box of concrete in front of his apartment that makes Andreas miss North Carolina, despite the myriad of bad memories there. He did not expect to have so many bad memories: Between the Mile High Swinging Bridge and the confrontation with Geneva, North Carolina could be considered the worst part of their trip. Andreas does not consider North Carolina to be the worst part of their trip, though. To him, the worst is yet to come. He did not expect to have so many bad memories in North Carolina. He expects, however, to have bad memories with his father. What can he possibly do to make up for the years of rote cards? How can he possibly justify leaving his sons with a mother who thinks them incapable of anything? Andreas is used to being hurt, though. That is not what makes what is to come the worst. The worst thing is that York does not expect to be burned. He thinks fire will make him immune to lava.

"We told Dad to expect us." York pushes the doorbell button. "I sure hope he—"

The door swings open, revealing a portly man with thinning brown hair and blue eyes that seem to have absorbed the gray of the city. "Boys!" He wraps his muscular arms around them, and York and Andreas alike jolt and wiggle out of the suffocating hold. "Are you ready to explore the city?"

"Actually, Dad," York starts. "The roads, once you get up to around here, get really busy and really stressful. I'm sure New York City is great, but we're too tired to go out today." He looks down at Andreas with a smile. "Wouldn't you ag—"

"Tired, schmired!" the man barks. "And no need to call me Dad! You're a man now yourself, Yorktown! Man to man, I'm Harlow."

Andreas blinks confusedly. Yorktown? York was named after New York, the state their mother is from, the state they're in right now!

"York," his brother echoes, in disbelief himself. "My name is just York. Yorktown is the name of the final battle of the American Revolution."

"Well, I know that," Harlow guffaws. "Didn't your mother tell you that I was in the Navy?" Andreas doesn't think the Navy was in the American Revolution... "Now then! Time's a wasting!" He grabs their bags from them and tosses them into the apartment carelessly.

Valuables, schluables, Andreas thinks morosely. Then, Harlow marches off, ordering them along.

Their father introduces them to the subway: the worst form of transportation. It is like a normal train, except it is underground, so the only view is of the gleaming eyes of rats, and there is no air to filter out the stench of urine. Yes, even in the subway train itself.

Once they exit the subway, the crowds, unfortunately, do not abate, but the smells do, and, as a result, Andreas is left able to admire for the first time the compact structure of the city. The gray skyscrapers and brown-bricked apartments evoke a sense of efficient stacking and organization: The people stay in one place, the businesses stay in another, and the green stuff—Andreas has seen one park so far—stays in a different place.

Their father tells them that Manhattan is just like a grid, except there are random curves in it, and their father does not allow them to stay on any single path, instead ushering them along like they are in a marathon, rapid-fire shouting the names of landmarks: "The Financial District: where the bigwigs work! Broadway: home to the best theaters in the world! The Empire State Building! Across the sea, Yorktown, there she is: Lady Liberty."

Andreas is actually interested in all of the landmarks, but between their father's busker-like breezing-by of any real details, the quick pace he's forcing them to maintain, and the seemingly equally fast speed of the throng all around them, Andreas is reminded of Las Vegas, except, unlike there, he is swept under the water, left gasping for air.

He imagines that he would swim no better than that bulldog over there. Between their father's rambling, Andreas points. York gasps—and for good reason.

Not only are purebred bulldogs rare, but the bulldog, which is gray with white blotches—or is it white with gray blotches?—is being pulled by a toddler: a toddler without any immediately visible adult supervision, which York comments on.

"*You're an adult,*" Andreas reminds his brother quietly, turning the volume on his tablet down.

"I also have no experience with toddlers!" York hisses back.

"*You had experience with me.*"

"You're my brother! It's different!" York insists. Even so, as the bulldog's leash gets tangled around the child's legs, York dives into action, disentangling the little boy. "You don't want to fall, do you? Or your dog?"

The little boy stares at him. Andreas is prepared to cover his ears just in case the toddler starts to wail. Instead of crying, though, the little boy's face splits into a grin as he points at York and shouts, "Da!"

York reddens. "Oh, no, I'm not your—"

Andreas follows the tiny finger to a man with a very fancy suit that appears to have been recently disheveled. The man seems to melt into his shoes as he sees his son. "Oh, thank goodness! You found him! You turn around for just a second, and your surprisingly fast kid can run off with your miraculously-now-average-speed dog!"

York, putting two and two together, looks relieved that he does not need to have a new little brother. "The miracle of life?" he offers, trying to calm the man down.

The man isn't really calm, though, until he has his son in his arms and his dog's leash tied around his wrist. "That it is." He looks at the little boy. "John, what do you say to the nice people who helped you?" The little boy coos, not understanding. The man shakes his head. "Well, I'll say it, since he can't." He nods to York and Andreas. "Thank you."

"John!" the toddler repeats.

"Yes, that is your name!" his da confirms. "And mine!"

"Wait, you have the same name?" Andreas asks. A spike of horror drives through him as he imagines being named "Harlow" or "Nova." What an unfortunate thing, to be named after your parents! What if someone calls your name and you both turn around?

The man nods. "I'm John Lowry. He's John Lowry…"

York points at the bulldog. "He's John Lowry?" he guesses.

"No!" Andreas retorts. *"The dog's name is Spartan Capital!"* Indeed, it was very nice of the John Lowrys to label their dog with the neon green bandana. Andreas wonders if he should have given Atlas a page from an atlas to wear.

John Lowry the man laughs. "No, no, my dog's name is Buddy! Spartan Capital is the name of my company!"

This time, it is York's turn to ask a question. "Wait, you have a comp—"

"Boys!" Their father's voice reverberates through the crowd. "Boys! Keep up with the tour!"

Andreas starts to move off in the direction of the call, but when he doesn't hear York's footsteps behind him, he looks back. York is watching John Lowry the man walking off with John Lowry the toddler, nodding at the little boy's incomprehensible babbling as if it were a Hollywood blockbuster.

"Boys! I'm crossing the street!" Harlow hollers.

"Uh…Which one?" York shouts into several throngs of pedestrians.

"This one!" It is the most unhelpful, least-labor-intensive answer possible, so it is the answer they get.

Desperate to not engage with New York City traffic—on foot or amongst cars—as much as possible, York jumps from the curb to where the cars are waiting at the red light without touching each other—unlike the people huddled together on the crosswalk. It is a mistake. He trips. He makes it to the other side of the street, but not without blood running down his hands, which he used to cushion the blow against the asphalt.

Andreas does not want to take any blow against the asphalt, so he waits by the crosswalk, waving his arms around him to try to ensure some distance between him and the other pedestrians.

By the time Andreas crosses the street, their father has registered the injury and is denying it—"Walk it off like a man"—and the crowd, while not stopping, stares on their way. A few even shoot glares at the man who is yelling at his bleeding son.

Andreas isn't under any misconception that York's pleas and blood are what prompt their father to drag his sons back to the apartment.

"You're no fun," Harlow grumbles.

Fun? As if the purpose of their trip is to entertain him?

* * *

They call it The City That Never Sleeps. New York City's reputation is accurate. Once again, the maps tell the truth. On the pull-out couch in his father's house, Andreas looks across the barrier of pillows erected between them at his brother. Brown hairs are starting to poke out across his upper lip. He will notice in the morning when he's taking off his retainers. Andreas had braces once, but he wasn't following the rules—no candy, the rule that almost did York in, and no picking at the wires: the rule that did do Andreas in—and they were expensive, so it wasn't worth the price.

Andreas is good at following rules. It was just that the braces rules were painful! York used to talk about the retainers being painful. Now, he doesn't talk about them in any capacity. Getting used to pain, though, doesn't mean that it's gone.

As Andreas slips on his sneakers, he swears he sees a pair of gleaming green eyes staring back at him. When he blinks, though, they're gone. The boy sighs. Ghosts are real. No need to be dramatic about it. A ghost is just a fragment of what was left behind. The real pain comes when you try to deny it.

He has a spare pair of shorts, but as he steps outside, it occurs to Andreas that people in the Northeast live in terrible cold, even in the summer. He's not going to take pants—his brother didn't pack any either, and he certainly isn't going to wear pants that belong to his father—but he's heard that the girls at school trade shirts all the time. He steps back into the apartment, to look for one of his father's sweatshirts to borrow.

Clothes go in the drawer. That's the rule. But maybe it's just a California rule because it seems that his father piles his shirts on a chair next to his bed. As he extracts the one on the bottom, the man snorts.

Andreas is prepared to laugh at himself with him, to lament his strangeness, but, strangely, his father goes back to sleep. As he slips on the sweatshirt—aptly named because if he were wearing it at home, he'd be sweating—he snorts again. Andreas gasps in recognition when the snort spasms into a snore. His mother snores when she's sick! (Even when she denies that she's sick.)

He will get him some medicine on the way back. The big pharmacies have 24/7 service.

In the bathroom, he closes the door and turns on the lights to pick out his first destination. He tuts as he studies his options. His mother had talked about how their father had moved to New York City, but The Bronx isn't even mostly in

Long Island! And all the "must-sees" Harlow showed them? In Long Island!

According to the borough maps Harlow got him, there is a 24-hour bus stop at Morris Park Avenue and Williamsbridge Road. Andreas peeks out the window: cat's eye Venus is against an inky black backdrop tonight, like the bottom of the sea. Maybe he shouldn't go out tonight? No. There will be less people out at night, even in The City That Never Sleeps, surely. Even if people aren't sleeping at this time of night, they are most likely at home. Or in someone's apartment. No, this is the only time he'll get to actually *see* any of the hallmarks of the movies he watches, not just get yelled at about them—and by the man who was crammed into their schedule without his permission, no less! This road trip is not about York and Andreas and the father that they never see. It is about York and Andreas!

Despite his anger at his brother, though, Andreas would have invited York to come along, if not for the fact that he got hurt on this tour. If Andreas drew blood at the Statue of Liberty, he would not hurry back. And it was Harlow's fault that York got hurt in the first place. If he allowed them to move slower, York would not have tripped! No, he is going alone. If he is going to learn anything about the backgrounds of fuzzy lighting and swelling music, it is better that he goes by himself anyway. Neither brothers nor fathers are romantic.

Andreas trots out of the brick building, noting with confusion that the lights in his father's neighbor's house still appear to be on. The city itself may not sleep, but surely the people do. Considering where he is on Tomilson Avenue, it would be quicker for him to go south then north to get to the bus stop, but that doesn't mean that he isn't tempted to sneak a peek.

Andreas peers through the open window. An old woman is in front of a bright, loud television. He can't hear the exact words that are coming from the television, but he can hear the volume and pitch—he hears an argument. The old woman wails at the television and buries her nose in an already-mostly-used tissue.

Well, that was disappointing, Andreas judges. Eager to make up for the sad scene, the boy crosses the street. Hadn't his father said something about a local museum? Looking on his map, however, he doesn't see anything that fits that description. He turns onto Judge Benjamin F. Nolan Way. Straight shot to the bus station from here. And what luck: There's a CVS on the way!

A door behind him flies open. At his jolt, the figure in the doorway introduces himself. "Name's Dormi...Y'know, of the funeral home?" A rotund man with salt-and-pepper hair jabs a bent finger back at the sign. At Andreas's expression—whatever it is—he cocks his head in confusion. "You not from 'round here, kid?"

Stranger danger...But someone who works in a funeral home hardly wants more work. Especially one that—lo and behold—bears his name.

"What you doing out so late?" Dormi asks.

Questions, questions. Well, Andreas has a question of his own: Can't he just...leave? Opting not to answer—not "ignoring," because ignoring is rude, whereas deciding not to answer is an appropriate response to a stranger—the boy continues down the street.

Oh, there's a CVS.

After buying some generic cold medicine, the boy goes back into the night. Up the street, no Dormi the funeral man. Down the street, no Dormi. No Dormi except the funeral home.

But a funeral home can't chase him.

The boy continues up the street and plops down on the bench in front of the bus stop, beside a fresh wad of gum that takes up too much of the bench.

He is confused about the gum. Why would someone stick their gum to the top of a public bench when there is a trash can right next to it? And who is chewing gum so late at night? Andreas doesn't like gum. If he's going to have something in his mouth, he has to eat it. That's the rule. It's bad to eat food late at night. It's even worse to eat not-food at night.

The boy winces at the pair of headlights approaching. He stands up to present his payment, but as the black spots in his vision from the artificial brightness are washed out in the night's ocean-blue, he realizes that one, what has pulled up is a car, not a bus, and two, the car has pulled up across the street.

A man gets out of the car. *"Dormi?"* Andreas asks through the tablet. Really, he's not that far from the funeral home. Was it really necessary for him to *drive* to find him?

He sees it on the top of the car, under the streetlight: a bar of red and blue lights. Andreas can't breathe. He feels the police officer's arms around him, yelling at him to calm down, but how can he be calm when a grown man with a gun is holding him down? Has anyone being squished into the ground ever been calmed down? Has any normal person ever been told to calm down while staring at a gun? Andreas can't breathe. The future is choking him.

"What are you doing out so late, son?" It always starts with a simple question that calls for a simple answer. The answer is never simple, though. The reason why he felt for her wasn't simple. The reason why they met wasn't simple. The reason why Raleigh killed herself wasn't simple. Has a normal person ever answered a question like that simply? "Do your parents know you're here, son?"

Okay, that question, admittedly, has a simple answer, but Andreas knows that "no" is never the answer a police officer wants to hear, so he tells him yes with a tiny, unthreatening nod.

"You're lying, son. You can't look me in the eye."

Oh, he's lying all right, but not because of that. It's a sloppy mistake, though. If he doesn't look at the gun, maybe the man will forget that he has it.

"You're going to have to come with me, son." He'll have to take a look at his map somewhere else. He needs to leave *now*. Andreas knows where the police officer will take him.

He will take him to the room where everyone can ignore his screams.

CHAPTER 13

———

People will ignore him, just like they ignored Atlas's death knell. He has met many strangers: Dormi the funeral man, Kit the CVS receptionist, even John the missing person. This is the first stranger he's felt in danger from. The police officer has a gun. Andreas has a box of cold medicine.

It's a start. Andreas throws the CVS bag at the police officer. It glances off him harmlessly but harming him wasn't the point. Harming him would be bad. (The boy wonders if the man with the gun would agree.) The glance that the police officer gives to the bag is not a glance he gives to Andreas. The boy breaks away.

He isn't under any ideas that he will win a fight, but he knows that he can run.

He tears to the left. The police officer is screaming. That's not good. People won't ignore *him*. But that's also good. The police officer is screaming because he is faster than him! The boy runs one block, two blocks, three blocks. As he runs, the houses behind him light up his back.

At the fourth block, the houses are lit in front of him, so he catches the sign. He whips his head to the side. Home Avenue?

The glance that he gives to the sign is not a glance that he gives to the road ahead. The boy slips and falls. Andreas feels blood bloom like mushrooms across his exposed legs. Just like in the movies, the mushrooms sap his strength. He starts to rise despite that, but, suddenly, his face is smushed against the asphalt by the police officer's large, sweaty hands, which press into his cheek, pushing him down.

"You have the right to remain silent. Anything you say may be used against you in a court of law."

It occurs to Andreas that he has no choice but to remain silent. At some point, he dropped his tablet.

He closes his eyes. Maybe if he stays perfectly still, the police officer will think he's roadkill. Then it will be unnecessary for him to use his gun.

He grunts as fire blazes behind his eyelids. He breaks his role. He yowls as he registers what's burning his retinas: a set of headlights! He doesn't really want to become roadkill! He tries to twist out of the way, but he is a twelve-year-old boy, and there is a man with a gun on top of him.

The headlights cut out. Another predator has already claimed this kill. Or maybe it's not convinced. Andreas thinks it can hear his heart continuing to flee.

"Skippy!" The voice is an illusion: a mirage conjured by his panicked fantasy. But as the shadow materializes in his field of view, Andreas realizes that this really *is* his brother. Not in the least because York identifies himself as such.

"That's my brother!" York shouts.

"Well, your brother is under arrest," the man on top of Andreas states. "He's a suspect in local gang activity."

Andreas can't properly emote, as smushed as he is, but his brother does that for him. "Local gang activity? Sir, neither of us live here."

"Oh, I know you're not from Morris Park. You're from one of the other neighborhoods." What does that even mean? Just because you live near a park, you can't be part of a gang?

"No, sir," York insists. "My brother and I don't live in the city. If you look it up, you can see that we live in Ridgecrest, California. I'm York Seaver. I'm nineteen. I'm going to The College of St. Rose in the fall. He's Andreas Seaver. He's twelve. He goes to James Monroe Middle School."

Somehow, the man doesn't seem convinced of any of it. Least of all…"He's twelve?"

"Yes, sir."

At this point, their father strides out of the car with all the practiced casualness of a military man. Andreas wonders what took him so long. Was he thinking it would be *fun* to experience being behind bars? The man with the gun recognizes him as one of his own. "Harlow?"

"Sorry about my boys, Warren," Harlow sighs. Because intervening to stop a false arrest is so not *fun*.

"These are the boys your ex-wife sent over?" At Harlow's nod, the man sitting on top of him stops doing that. York rushes over, crouching next to him, placing himself between the boy and the officer. His back is away from the gun. Andreas stands up hastily, never letting his gaze leave it.

It is only once he is standing, ready to run should the need arise (having realized that this is Hone Avenue, not Home Avenue) that he realizes that his brother had his back to the police officer so his hands could face him.

Andreas's hands swat away the remaining asphalt in the cuts on his legs. The asphalt, ceaselessly black, like the gun that is still at the police officer's side, peels off his skin like a shell, revealing the angry, red injuries underneath, even as the police officer responsible for those injuries chats easily with their father, who has the standard speech: They're country boys, they're curious, they were raised by a wench—

Andreas doesn't realize that he hasn't said anything about him not understanding until the police car has disappeared into the blue shell of night.

Their father stops waving. "Okay! Back to the house, boys!"

Andreas whimpers. His tablet is still missing, the tablet Dad gave him...Does he not care about it now that it's no longer a *fun* gift?

"That's it?" York hisses.

Andreas glances at him in confusion. It's true, he can hardly believe that he made it out of that encounter without being locked in some sort of room, but that's it.

"Warren wouldn't hurt him." It isn't that dark. They're under a streetlight. Surely his father can see the cuts on his legs and the bruise on his face (or the bruise that is his face). When he talked to the police officer, did he not see the gun or the manacles?

"Except he did," York presses. "Do you think Andreas smashed his own face into the street?"

"You'll be *fine*."

Of course, they'll be fine. As long as they're fine, it's still fun. As long as it's still fun, their father does not need to consider their opinions. They're just props to his circus. He's trying to convince both of them that his fun is their fun: no puzzling over what to do necessary.

In another place, Andreas would have drunk up those words like a parched traveler. Now, he sees that the water that his father is offering him is tainted. He's not fine. He thought he was going to get shot! Has any normal person been told that they're fine after seeing their life flash before their eyes?

"Don't tell me about fine!" York shouts. "You said fine

when I told you that Andreas wanders. You said fine when I told you to hide the door keys. You said fine when I screamed at you to wake up because Andreas was gone!" He points at his brother. "What about a twelve-year-old that you're responsible for getting tackled in the middle of the street to get arrested is *fine* to you?"

"He's fine now."

York turns to him. "Are you fine, Andreas?" The boy shudders at the intensity of his name. His brother's voice rumbles like an earthquake.

Their father doesn't brace himself. "You're coddling him! Boys will be boys!"

"Boys will be *killed!*" York roars back. "Boys like him will get killed!"

Andreas recoils. He knows that his brother is correct, but he has cast him out alone. Something about that…isn't correct. Recognizing his volume, the young man sobers. He silently hovers his arm over him. Andreas snuggles up to that arm: recognition that they're leaving the circus together. "Come on," York says. "We're staying at a hotel." On the way to the hotel, they retrace Andreas's steps, but the tablet has receded into the night tide.

* * *

"What in the world does he think this is?" York's snarl seems like the vestiges of a nightmare.

Andreas awakens with a pained groan. He tosses and turns in his bed, not wanting to get up yet. He shoots into a sitting position with a startled yelp, however, as he catches himself in the mirror across from the bed, registering the mottled patchwork of colors that is his face: a sea of blue and purple. He likes both colors individually. He even thinks they look nice together. Just…not on him. He sniffles in alarm because now the threat of the gun and the manacles and being smushed on the street is inescapable. He can't escape his face!

"Skippy?" York steps into their bedroom in the hotel—two twin-sized beds, sectioned off from the rest of their space by a curtain—and the box he is holding clatters to the ground. "Hang on, I'll get you an ice pack." He pauses to consider what he is looking at. "Or two?" he asks.

Andreas shakes his head and holds up one finger. York nods and scampers off to the bathroom, a curtain and door away. He needs a free hand, after all, to examine this box… Andreas slides off the bed and puts the box on top of the sheets. The box is wrapped in paper that is white with the phrase *Get well soon!* in red repeated throughout.

When York returns, Andreas shows the wrapping paper to him. "Hmph," the young man scoffs. "As if he doesn't know what happened." He spins the box in his hands, finding a tag. "*To: The Boys,*" York reads out loud. He looks at his younger brother. "Should we both tear into it, then?"

Andreas figures that is the fairest thing to do. He nods.

"Okay, then. In three, two, one…*Pull!*"

They rip the wrapping paper apart with tugs in the opposite direction. Another box falls out between them, landing on the sheets of Andreas's bed. Andreas pulls a small, black rectangle out of the box. He fumbles at the switches on the side, but, ah yes, it lights up.

"A new tablet…" York breathes, as Andreas starts going through the set-up screens. He pulls the packaging toward him and spots something sticking out from underneath it. He tears off a piece of paper from the bottom of the box.

"*Yorktown,*" York begins to read out loud. "*I should have kept a better eye on your brother. The Big Apple's sunk its teeth into so many adventurous young people, and I should have known that he would be no exception. This is the latest tablet. The old thing he had before could barely run two tabs, am I right?"* York blinks. "And that's the end," he breathes. He flips the paper over, then, in desperation, turns it upside down. "Where's the rest of it?"

York waits patiently for his brother's voice to return. When it does, it comes with Andreas's frown. *"If only this were an online document,"* the boy laments. *"Then we could search for the word* sorry.*"*

York shakes his head. "No need. Zero results." He hands the paper over to Andreas, so he can check for himself.

Indeed, no *sorry*. Not even an *Andreas*.

"Yorktown isn't your name," Andreas states.

"I know!" York snaps. "I was not named after some battle! I was named after the state! Where he and Mom met! Where we are right now!"

Andreas flinches at the volume. He picks up the ice pack and rubs one of his swollen cheeks. The only thing that is the right color is his scar... *"I'm sorry that you're angry."*

His brother deflates. "Skippy, I'm not angry at *you*. Yes, you shouldn't have gone alone into the city at night, but I thought you might, so I told myself and Dad to keep an eye on you. Which we didn't do. And because of that, that police officer almost—" York curls over his curdling stomach. "That's not your fault, though."

"It's not your fault either!" Andreas insists, scooting up to his brother. *"You didn't push me into the crosswalk!"*

"True," York admits. "But I understood what you might do. He didn't. Which is no excuse, but..." He shakes his head. "This sounds wrong, but."

"But?"

At Andreas's prompting, he continues. "There's you and me. We understand each other. Then there's the rest of the world. They seem to understand each other fine too. But then there's you and me and the rest of the world. Then, it's like we're on opposite sides of a bridge. We've always been told that we're the ones who aren't communicating. That we need to use our words—" His gaze drifts down to the tablet. "—or look at people's eyes. We've always been told that we're the ones who are wrong."

Andreas smiles, although it makes his face ache. *"Well, we've also been told that you can't go to college. Which is wrong. We've been told that we'd never make it across the country. Wrong. And, most recently, we were told that the police officer wouldn't hurt me."* He waves a hand around his face. *"Very wrong."*

York's eyes widen. "So, Dad's apology…"

"This non-apology," Andreas corrects.

"This non-apology is wrong."

Andreas nods. *"Although you hardly need to tell me that. In fact, I think you told our father that too."*

York stands up and spins his memory, twirling in rewind, echoing his assertion from the previous night: "What about a twelve-year-old that you're responsible for getting tackled in the middle of the street to get arrested is *fine* to you?"

Andreas flinches again at the retort, but, in the safety of the sunlight, he feels a thrill at the assertiveness in York's voice. It is the assertiveness of an adult. York stops, and as he blinks to recover his sense of direction, he picks up his phone with a clear sense of purpose. Andreas cranes his neck to read what he is typing. It is a text message to their father. Andreas reads: "We are not coming back to you. We are finishing our journey on our own. You did not keep Andreas safe, and you did not take responsibility for your mistake. I am taking responsibility for the mistake of coming to you. If you want to talk about how mistaken I am, you can tell Mom all about it." York gives their father their mother's phone number.

Andreas gives an approving, poking-tongue smile to his brother. York's face reddens, yet he still straightens up, perhaps embarrassed at the attention but not intimidated into doubting his decisions. "Well then!" York pipes up. "What do you want to do now, Skippy?"

CHAPTER 14

———

Andreas flops back against the pillows of his hotel bed. *"We need to get to your school before my face turns green,"* he decides, holding his new tablet over his head, looking at pictures of bruises. *"My face could look like this in five days!"* he presses, sitting back up and pushing the tablet into his brother's face. *"Would a guard let that face into a school?"*

York inches closer to the screen, settling onto his brother's bed, looking torn between throwing up and wanting to hug the poor soul in the picture. "This guy got tackled by a police officer too, it looks like," he decides, straddling the line by hugging his stomach.

Andreas draws the tablet back toward him. *"Really?"* He skims the article and then reads the comments. *"It looks like Dad isn't the only one who can't believe what they see right in front of them."* Andreas has no empathy for those in such deep denial, though. At some point, you must go back to your life in the real world and hope they catch up.

Andreas looks up the name of York's school. The College of Saint Rose is real. His brother worked really hard to get in. He really can't wait to see it!

York calls out from the hallway. "If we want to beat the face-clock, you're going to need to help me pack, Skippy!"

* * *

"Oh, oh! I recognize this building from my online tour! This is the EAC!"

"The what?" Andreas asks, pressing his face against the window.

"The sports building," York corrects hastily. "Rather, the Events and Athletics Center. Thus, EAC." Like Meredith College, the College of St. Rose features, primarily, brick buildings, but, unlike Meredith College, the College of Saint Rose has buildings—including this "EAC"—that have walls entirely made of glass. Andreas thinks that might be because the trees are farther away from the buildings, so looking out the glass doesn't just reveal a wall of bark. Since most of the buildings are not accessible to him, Andreas, honestly, prefers the fusion look of Meredith College. Considering that York is not looking out for danger here, though, he still prefers the College of Saint Rose.

"I don't care what you're calling it! You're driving away from it!"

"This isn't student parking, Skippy!"

Once their car is safely situated in student parking, the duo backtracks their way to the Events and Athletics Center. "So...sports," York resumes, trying to recapture his train of thought.

"What position will you be playing?" York jolts. *"In soccer,"* Andreas prompts. *"You've played soccer in Ridgecrest for four years! That's impressive!"*

York blushes. "It's, uh, really not. Not for a D2 school."

"*Wh-What do you mean?*" the boy demands. His brother is great at soccer! He blocked that last-minute play from the other team!

"I'll explain inside," York says gently. "There's a Starbucks inside. Do you want anything?"

"*I don't want chocolate chip cookies!*" Andreas yelps.

"For your information, I wasn't going to get chocolate chip cookies. I was going to get a blueberry muffin."

Andreas blinks rapidly. His brother? Turning down a chance to stock up on chocolate? Did the wrong person get back into the car at EddieWorld? Regardless, Andreas has a question. "*May I have a blueberry muffin too?*"

* * *

York makes their order—two blueberry muffins, one orange juice, and one water—to a barista who looks like they have sampled too much of the coffee. Then, he lets Andreas pick their table since the Starbucks is mostly empty. Andreas picks a small table in the corner, next to the window. A trophy case rests across the hallway. York has won trophies. Why can't he win trophies here?

"*So why can't you play soccer?*" Andreas demands. "*What makes a D2 so special?*"

"First of all—" York is quick to correct. "—it's not that I can't play soccer. They haven't *banned* it. I just can't play on their main team."

"*I think that's dumb,*" Andreas states.

"Your opinion is noted, but you are not a D2 school."

Who cares about some school's opinion? Schools are just empty buildings if people have the opinion that they don't want to go there! "*What is a D2 school?*" the boy demands.

"A D2 school is…in the middle. Not as good as a D1 school but not as bad as a D3 school. D2 schools kind of fly under the radar in that way. Coach Diego told me that I could have gotten on a D3 team—"

"So why didn't you?"

York falls quiet, nursing his orange juice. Andreas looks down at the water rippling in his cup from his shouting. Ah. He has been asking the wrong question. If the school isn't stopping York from playing soccer, then there is only one reason that he is not doing it. *"Are you sad that you can't play soccer on their main team?"*

"No," York answers with certainty. "I'm sad that I'm going to be so far—"

A head of curly red hair, wrapped around a freckled face, pops between them, having gotten up from a table a few feet away to, apparently, state her own opinion. "Well, that's a harsh way to describe college sports, isn't it?" The young woman, a few years older than York, rests her face against her knuckle.

"I…I didn't mean any offense!" York squeaks, going pale.

The young woman guffaws. "Hey, I'm not a student-athlete!" She raises her hands, no more fist to be found. "No need to worry! As long as you don't disrespect the School of Math and Sciences, we're good!"

Andreas looks between the new arrival and his brother confusedly. *"I thought we were in The College of Saint Rose?"*

York smiles at the boy reassuringly. "We are. The College of Saint Rose has four schools: the School of Business, the School of Math and Sciences, the School of Arts and Humanities, and the School of Education. It's a pretty common thing for colleges with a lot of students to have multiple 'schools.'"

The young woman nods. "Our School of Business is called Huether, for Richard J. Huether, a trustee who donated a lot of money toward the school's construction. Our School of Education also has a more formal name: the—" She taps the table with her finger as she speeds through the name, squeezing her eyes shut, as if to force the memory out of them. "—Thelma P. Lally School of Education." Her eyes fly open, sparking with pride at her own recall. "She worked as a teacher for many years and donated a lot of money toward hospitals and schools in the Albany area."

York's eyes widen in awe. "Wow, how do you know that? Are you from admissions or something?"

She laughs. "As a matter of fact, I do work in admissions! OL and all."

Andreas groans. *"Can you use fullllll words?"* He puts in too many *l*s in his tablet, so the word *full* will be drawn out.

"Oh, sorry! I'm an *Orientation Leader,"* she exclaims. "It's been drilled into me to use the 'lingo,' you know?" She looks between the duo, resting her chin against her knuckle again, index finger poking out as she points at them questioningly. "Are you new students?"

"I am," York says. "My name is York Seaver, and this is my little brother, Andreas."

"You're a little early for orientation!" she gasps. "But, in a way, I can make this a practice orientation if you'd like! Oh, and I'm Buffy, by the way."

"Buffy?" Andreas yelps. He scrolls through his tablet furiously and shows her the picture. *"Like the vampire slayer?"*

The young woman's laughter comes out in an unapologetic snort. "I love that show, but…No. Buffy like the buffalo. The Cape buffalo—*Syncerus caffer caffer*—to be exact."

As his brother hums in confusion, Andreas looks up a picture and shows it to York. "Wow," he breathes. "They're *huge!"*

"Both of my parents are zookeepers," Buffy explains. "And there were several animals under their care that were pregnant at the same time my mom was. They decided to make it a game: Whichever animal gave birth closest in time to my mom, they needed to reference the animal in the baby's name! The Cape buffalo won. Personally, though, I'm a little bit upset that the Bengal tiger didn't win. Look them up! Aren't they magnificent?"

Andreas remembers that tigers are also common mascots. He looks up the College of Saint Rose's mascot.

York peers over his shoulder, recognizes the knight-themed mascot suit, and chuckles. "Guess what he just looked up?"

Andreas harrumphs, disappointed. What kind of college puts a guy in a costume that is just a guy in a costume?

"Fear, The Golden Knight? Don't tell my bosses at admissions, but I don't like him either. I always prefer a good old-fashioned animal mascot. I can't tell you how disappointed my parents were when they found out about Fear! 'Knights don't live in a zoo!'" she whispers conspiratorially. "I don't think a lot of the alums like him either. His design wasn't finalized until 2001, and the costume is new too! They're not subtle about it either! I've seen *several* alums come through Moran Hall just to protest about 'Who is that in the pictures?'"

"*Moran Hall?*" Andreas asks.

"I'll show you!" Buffy chirps. As she stands up, Andreas realizes that while her red, curly hair is short, Buffy is actually tall, clocking in at five feet and ten inches. Somehow, her freckles, those little dots, made her seem smaller. "Although there isn't much to see there if your professors don't have offices there. Are you planning on studying History?"

Buffy turns so she is walking backward mid-stride as she cuts through the grass and onto the pavement. Andreas is impressed. Does being an OL teach you that skill? What kind of other amazing things will York learn at this college?

"So you don't want to study history. I showed you Scanlan Hall, but you're already admitted, so why should you care?" Buffy sighs, pressing her fingers against each other in a steeple-shape—or like the shape of all the roofs Andreas has seen so far—under her chin. "No. I think I'm going about this the wrong way. If this is a Practice Orientation, I need to be practicing too, practicing listening to what the students under my wing need from me." Andreas stoops down at the sound of chittering. "York, what do you need to see before Orientation?"

Andreas stops from where he is pondering a fat squirrel. As he turns, the squirrel steals the offering of blueberry muffin between them. The boy sighs, but he can summon a squirrel again. All he needs is another blueberry muffin, and there are plenty of Starbucks around. York, on the other hand, only has one opportunity to explore what he needs to explore before Orientation.

York is aware of the opportunity, but the enormity of the things he needs to see overwhelms him. Still, there is one thing he can identify, within the pile. "I've been told that I will be living in—" He takes out his phone, navigating to the confirmation email, walking in a circle to wind up his memory. "—Brubacher Hall?"

"Oh, Bru!" Buffy exclaims. "I lived in Bru my first year too!" She scurries ahead of the brothers. "Follow me. It's on State Street!"

Buffy leads them to a brick building with white pillars—huh, Andreas thinks, do colleges just think brick buildings with white pillars are the smartest looking buildings? The boy loses interest in that question, though, as a slimmer squirrel climbs up one of the pillars.

Buffy scans her student ID and holds the door for the duo. When she sees the boy dawdling, she snickers. "Come on, Andreas! The squirrels will still be here when we're done inside! In fact, there's something inside Bru that can help you with them..."

Intrigued by the promise of claiming his rightful throne as king of the squirrels—as well as seeing where his brother is going to live—Andreas scampers in.

"Welcome to Bru!" Buffy exclaims. "Here, York, you will be living alongside 304 other first-year students, as well as 11 RAs!"

"How do you get that number?" Andreas asks.

"Because that's the number of people we can fit in this building! College students are quite capable of living in small spaces." She gasps. "Wait! I shouldn't have said that! I *can't* say that at Orientation!"

York laughs. "The truth is safe with us. Isn't that right, Skippy?" Andreas plays the sound effect of a zipper closing. He doesn't like the feeling of zippers, but he likes the sound of them!

Buffy grins. "Perfect! York, are you planning on studying Art?"

York frowns. "No. I'm sorry, I said no to History too. The truth is, I don't really know what I want to study yet."

Buffy comes to York's side. "No need to worry! It's perfectly normal to not know what you want to study yet! You know you don't need to declare your major until the spring of next year, right?"

As Buffy shares about how normal it is to be indecisive—and being indecisive certainly is normal for York—Andreas studies the directory displayed on the wall. There appear to be professors' offices in this dorm building—Andreas wonders where *they* sleep if it is so cramped—but at least he knows where they eat. The boy points to the sign marking the entrance to *Brubacher Café*. "*They sell food here?*"

Buffy sighs as a memory crashes into her like a wave. "Shortly after I got re-assigned to a new roommate, I got sick. Nothing major, but I was *miserable*. The soups and sandwiches at the Café saved my life!"

"*Soups and sandwiches?*" Andreas turns around to York. "*I hope to see you eating soups and sandwiches when I come to see you here!*"

The color in York's face is pulled out of him like a tide. Andreas looks to Buffy for help, but the only hint she gives is a sad smile. "I'll leave you two alone."

* * *

York leaves Brubacher Hall in a hurry. "I need to talk to you somewhere that's not here. There are too many people here."

Even Andreas doesn't think there are that many people here—he's seen a few gray-haired professors trundling about, but that's it—but he knows that, sometimes, one pair of eyes staring at your back is too many eyes when you're feeling sad. And his brother certainly is sad. He just doesn't know *why*. They are in the college York is going to go to! They made a new friend! The squirrels are adorable!

Andreas finds that he doesn't care why his brother is sad as much as he cares about how he can help. He looks up a map of Albany. "*There is a park nearby. Beverwyck Park.*"

When he searches for pictures of Beverwyck, he is confused to find images of an old estate. *"Not to be confused with Beverwyck Manor! That's in Rensselaer!"*

He finds pictures of Beverwyck Park and is disappointed to see merely a baseball diamond surrounded by tall grass. York, however, seems pleased with the results. "Perfect. No one will be playing baseball today. Buffy says it's too hot."

Andreas cocks his head at his brother. *"It's only 85 degrees."*

York raises his arms. "I know! But Buffy says that's hot for around here!" Andreas shudders as he ponders what Buffy considers *cold*.

* * *

Beverwyck Park is even more disappointing than it is in the pictures: It's a baseball diamond surrounded by tall grass, but there aren't even any squirrels around!

York chuckles at his brother's pouting. "I've heard that the prettiest season around here is fall."

"Oh yeah?" Andreas snarks. *"Is that when it's not too hot?"*

"No clue!" York exclaims. "What I do know about, though, is the trees." He directs his little brother's attention to the line of trees marking the borders of the park. "In the fall, up in places like this, some trees' leaves change color!"

Andreas gapes at the pictures on York's phone: a hillside swathed in the reds, oranges, and yellows of a sunset in the middle of the day. It looks unmoored from time. But in Beverwyck Park right now, Andreas can hear the humming of bugs, the chimes of a faraway ice cream truck, and the spritzing of lawn sprinklers. He is firmly fastened to summer. That ethereal autumn is a faraway island on the ocean's horizon: an uninhabited mirage.

"*That's not real.*"

"Yes, it is!" York insists. "I'll send you pictures in, like, two months. You'll see! And you'll know they're not edited because you know I'm hopeless with art!"

Ah, and there it is again. "*Why can't I just see it for myself?*" Andreas broaches.

York sinks into the grass like a wilting flower. "I'm sorry," he murmurs.

Andreas hates the scratchiness of the grass on his bare knees and can hardly imagine the sensation of it on his exposed arms. He hates the weariness in his brother's voice more. "*You have nothing to be sorry for. It's not your fault the pictures look fake.*"

"They *do!*" he chokes out. "And I've been being fake too!"

Being fake means telling a lie. Andreas cannot think of any lie York has told him throughout the entire journey. Yes, he did not tell him about Geneva, but not telling someone about something that hurts is not lying. It's self-defense.

"This trip...was a lot," York begins. "A lot of thinking about planning, a lot of angering Mom, a lot of fun, and...a lot of money. Just like college. Andreas, you can't come and see me. Not in the fall. You'll see snow—and the pictures and videos I've seen of snow are equally unbelievable—when Mom comes to pick me up for winter break, but other than that..." He hugs his phone close to his chest. "We'll both be talking with our devices. I'll be here. You'll be there. With Mom. Without me." He sniffles. "I'm crying. I'm sad. That's what I'm sad about, Skippy. Not the D2 soccer team. I'm sad that I'm going to be so far away from you." He rubs his nose into his sleeve. "Sorry. I know I'm gross. But...may I touch you?"

It is quintessentially York: to be crying and still thinking of *Andreas's* comfort first. "*On a park bench. I don't like the grass.*"

York acquiesces, and the duo pile onto a park bench with a dead person's name on it with heavy, still-beating hearts. "I almost didn't do it, Skippy. Go to college, I mean. But this is something I need to do. If you're going to live with me, we need to live *somewhere*. But somewhere doesn't happen unless you go there—with money. College costs a lot of money, but this stupid little piece of paper that takes four years to get will let me *make* money. Four years, Skippy! That's longer than middle school! And middle school is *awful!*"

"*You're telling me.*" He's the one still stuck there!

"And the four years that I'll be here are four years that I'm not with you: eighth grade, ninth grade, tenth grade, and eleventh grade. You'll be a teenager when I'm done. A *teenager!* And I won't be!"

"*You'll be a real adult,*" Andreas types out slowly, reverently.

"And I'm *terrified* of that!" York confesses. "So...I had this idea, and Mom agreed, thinking it wouldn't happen: Before I go for four years, Skippy and I will get in a car and drive around for, what, four weeks? Four months? Whatever. Not important. The important thing is it'll be just the two of us, and he'll be in charge of where we go because he's had all these maps for seven years, and he hasn't been to *one* place on any of those maps!"

"*Las Vegas was lame.*"

"It was! But how could we have known that unless we went?" He takes a deep breath. "When I graduate, you will be sixteen years old."

Andreas gasps. "*Sixteen-year-olds can drive!*"

York blinks in shock. "You're...you're right. Oh, that's *perfect!* Yes, and we can drive again, looking for a place for us to live together. We'll have two years to decide. That point on the horizon is so *clear* to me, Skippy, but...for a long time,

I didn't know how to get there."

But there's the *but*. Something changed. Something changed while they were on this trip. *"But then what happened?"*

"This trip happened, and we went to the farthest-away college that accepted me. But before that…we talked to people. Without Mom. And it was still hard. That's not right. There's still a gap, and someone needs to build a bridge. I can build the bridge, Skippy. I can help people like you. People who can't talk or maybe they can, but the words don't come out right. I just want to do good, and this is one way where I already have an idea how: speaking out, making sure that people on the other side of the bridge look across and register that there are faces there, many faces."

People like York, charging into the ethereal hillside sunset of a Northeast autumn, an island that is so far away from where he has planted his roots. The York from back in Ridgecrest, California could not have been prepared for that new beginning and even the inevitable New England nightfall that they both know must exist beyond the fake-looking pictures of fall foliage and the smiling college brochures. That York needed to be convinced to uphold his end of the deal. That York wasn't sold on going to college yet. Andreas helped him. This trip—*his* trip, according to his brother—has helped him.

And Andreas knows that York will help so many people. No one ever truly outgrows their fear of the dark. So, he will wait for his brother: for four years, until he returns with a degree to certify his journey. For six years, until Andreas can legally join the journey York will begin here, in the capital of the state he was named after. This trip may have been his, but Andreas knows that the next adventure is all York's.

"You will," Andreas promises. *"People like you* always *help."*

ACKNOWLEDGEMENTS

———

Anyone who has ever told you that writing a book is easy has lied to you. Anyone who has ever told you that you can write a book by yourself has lied to you. The truth is that this difficult journey could not have been possible without these people: some of whom I knew before and some of whom I have met through this adventure. I will *All Ways* be grateful to...

Jules Pigott
Jane Leach
Kierra Coleman
Mary Coons
Mary Sheridan
Jennifer Sherman
Patricia McCarthy
Joanna Fracasso
Jennifer Capral
Beryl Roberts
Rebecca Coons
Amanda Capo
Claire Robertson

Noreen Simmons
Michael Kelly
Jennifer Lano
collin2322
Lindsey Restelli
Allison Pistolessi
Judy Brown
Jennifer Savage
Caroline Sears
Kim Monchik
Wendy Perreault
William Gabriel
Jennifer Knox

Beverly Wolf
Amanda Zaleski
Jeffrey Jasenski
Adam Brock
Laura Holt
John Lowry
Jill Linker
John Crosson
Katherine Roth
James Roth
Louis Peterson
Nathan Herzog
Linda Powers
Mary Horn
Maura Harris
William H Coons III
Richard Millington
Oliver Avery
Evelyn Cohen
Dimitri Yang
Alphonse J Forestandi Jr.
Jordan Karp
Ashley Lam
Scott Pawlich
Amy Bigelow
Elizabeth K Sanders
Pete Govert
Mary Murphy
William Petty
James Turner
Nancy Fall
Eric Koester

Deborah Newhouse
Fabiola Flores-Salazar
Nicholas Buckley
Donald Hunter
Julianna Tymoczko
Barbara Szymaszek
Gregory Morris
Ariana Stephen
Steve Nezas
Kailey Walters
Grace Gardner
Elizabeth Courtney
Marguerite Courtney
Sandra Manafort
Eli Mendoza
Warren Dotson
Emily Speight
Deborah Kreithen
April Cheever
Jennifer O'Brien
Anne Sandor
Matthew Dicks
Hazel Kalderon
Cory Frankiel
Joy Zhou
Daniel Zipadelli
Isabel Fitzsimons
Elizabeth Hurlburt
Rathan Enfused
Milton Ault III
Isabella Blake

Made in the USA
Middletown, DE
10 May 2021